G R JORDAN

The Culling at Singing Sands

A Highlands and Islands Detective Thriller

First edition

ISBN: 978-1-914073-60-1

This book was professionally typeset on Reedsy.
Find out more at reedsy.com

78% of people surveyed said they would rather die quickly than live in a retirement home

Contents

Foreword

This story is set in the areas of Inverness, the Cairngorms and the Isle of Eigg. Although incorporating known cities, towns and villages, note that all events, persons and specific places are fictional and not to be confused with actual buildings and structures which have been used as an inspirational canvas to tell a completely fictional story.

And I doubt anyone would get permission for a retirement home on the Isle of Eigg!

Acknowledgement

To Susan, Jean and Rosemary for your work in bringing this novel to completion, your time and effort is deeply appreciated.

Novels by G R Jordan

The Highlands and Islands Detective series (Crime)

1. Water's Edge
2. The Bothy
3. The Horror Weekend
4. The Small Ferry
5. Dead at Third Man
6. The Pirate Club
7. A Personal Agenda
8. A Just Punishment
9. The Numerous Deaths of Santa Claus
10. Our Gated Community
11. The Satchel
12. Culhwch Alpha
13. Fair Market Value
14. The Coach Bomber
15. The Culling at Singing Sands
16. Where Justice Fails

Kirsten Stewart Thrillers (Thriller)

1. A Shot at Democracy
2. The Hunted Child

Island Adventures Series (Cosy Fantasy Adventure)

1. Surface Tensions

Dark Wen Series (Horror Fantasy)

1. The Blasphemous Welcome
2. The Demon's Chalice

Chapter 1

Hope McGrath stood on the cliff path looking out into the blue water. It was not one simple colour, but a patchwork of hues with the occasional spray of white due to the choppiness of the surface. There was a stiff breeze blowing through her hair. Maybe that allowed her to let forth a small tear, blaming it on something in her eye.

Aunt Mary had been a go-getter. One of the family who'd seen life in its fullest. Hope remembered her as the auntie who told her as a young child that she could be anything. The woman had never married, but there had been men in her life as well for she had loved and lost on many different occasions on several continents, and yet she decided to come here to end it all. Here was where she had intended to spend the last days. Unfortunately, those days had not been that long.

The Isle of Eigg was something of an island paradise, as long as you were not expecting palm trees and piña coladas in the shade. Like most of the Scottish islands, it could get its fair share of rough weather, and while there was plenty of greenery, it had that savage look to it, untamed and wild. Then again, wasn't that Aunt Mary?

But islands like this also often had rare features. As Hope looked down to her left, she saw one of them. There was a sandy beach, which they said when you stood on it, made a noise like it was singing. Hope had researched it. It was something to do with the silica content, but that was rather drab compared to the tales of a shore that was alive. No doubt this would be one of the things that Aunt Mary would have enjoyed. Hope could have seen her bare-footed, twirling across the sand in all sorts of weather.

Turning around, Hope looked back down the path she'd walked along and saw cut into the hillside, 'The Singing Sands Later but Better Township'. It was a retirement home with a difference, there for people who didn't want to be stuck in a room, wheeled out to see the latest vicar that was coming with an uplifting sermon, but rather for those who wanted to live on the edge right until they fell off it. Hope had been excited when Aunt Mary had told her she was going there, but work had been so busy she had failed to get down to see her. Now it was too late.

Both eyes were now streaming tears and Hope let herself cry, away from everyone else right here on what felt like the edge of the world. They said that Aunt Mary had been on this very path; it was from here she'd fallen. Hope looked around trying to work out how. Sure, the weather could be rough at times, but to actually take someone over the small restraining barrier down towards the rocks and out to sea seemed unlikely.

Mary had gone for a walk that night and there was nothing unusual in it, wrapped up in her shawl, laughing, they said, as she went out the door, never to return. There'd been a light drizzle, making Hope think that the wind conditions that night had not been as bad as they'd been forecasted. There were no lights along the path as those who enjoyed this sort of scenery preferred it raw. She imagined her aunt standing here, feeling the wind biting into her face. Indeed, in her younger days, she might've run down to the beach, throwing all to the wind and jumped into the sea for a swim, although in her eighties she had slowed down a little. Maybe if she had a wet suit on, she might've gone for it.

Hope had arrived that day on the ferry over from Oban, some three weeks after the death of her aunt. On arrival, she'd been greeted by a young woman in her mid-twenties who'd offered her condolences to Hope and advised, as per instruction, there'd been a small ceremony and burial for Aunt Mary. Of course, there was no body in the casket which had been lowered into a grave and then covered back up again under the earth.

On arrival, Hope had wandered first to Aunt Mary's room and then burst down in floods of tears on seeing the number of photographs of herself, both as a young girl and now as the strapping and simply gorgeous detective sergeant she'd become. Those were her aunt's words, not hers. Although she hadn't seen her face to face for maybe a year, Hope had contacted her aunt several times, for they spoke maybe once a month. Usually, it was when Hope was feeling down and needed picked up, wanted to know what was the latest escapade from her aunt.

While in her aunt's room, she'd found the brochure for the home. When she said room, it really didn't do justice to what her aunt had. Each room was a house in itself. There was a kitchenette at one end, and in her aunt's room, a stunning four-poster bed in one corner. A TV and lounge were also there, as well as a balcony out to the sea. And yet amongst all this were buzzers, bells, alarms, anything to get attention if you felt ill or poorly. Her aunt had called it assisted living, but Hope, looking around the room, had thought of it only as really living.

Her aunt had never had children and so Hope had been the light of her eyes. When Hope's own parents had emigrated, Hope found a keen attachment to her aunt and seemed to talk to her more than she ever did to her own parents. Her own mother was not happy that Hope was in the murder squad, thinking her above that and more suitable to a glamorous role rather than the dogged investigation work she went through. But Aunt Mary had always praised her, always pushed her to try for more.

The little graveyard beyond the retirement home was beautifully cut out, with delicately arranged paths for what was not a busy graveyard. There were three headstones and in one corner was the one that was dedicated to Mary McGrath. Inscribed on the stone were the words 'All the better for seeing you,' a catchphrase of Aunt Mary's.

Hope had taken time to sit down in front of the grave and say some words to her aunt. She thought of the old woman laughing at her, asking her what she was doing here, having to say things when she could just talk to the open air. Her aunt believed she was everywhere in life and certainly in death, she felt she would go back. She was part of nature and to nature she would return. Inside, Hope desired that for her, but she felt suddenly very alone. Her one-time mentor was gone, the person who had guided her through her younger years, and that reassurance of someone who had gone before was now away as well.

It had been hard for Hope's partner, the rental car manager, to understand why she didn't want him to come with her. Things had been going well and she'd told Aunt Mary many times about the wonderful new man in her life. At times, Aunt Mary would ask questions that were slightly rude and probably required too much detail, but Hope loved her for it. The fact was that she always wanted the best for Hope, keen to know her niece was happy.

From the graveyard, Hope had walked down to the path that was above the singing sands beach. The path continued round, to a rock face that spectacularly overhung the sea below. Hope had been advised that was where her aunt had fallen from, although they'd no evidence to say which bit of it. In her heart, Hope prayed that the woman was pulling a blinder on them all and that she'd simply not liked the home and disappeared off to some other part of the world. But as Hope had come down to see this newish building, she could see why her aunt would come here. Hope put two hands on the railing and something inside her checked it was secure. It was solid. She allowed herself to lean on it and she dipped her head down and let go with the tears. For the next five minutes, she wept her heart out.

As she lifted her head, wiping her nose with the back of her hand, she peered down along the shore, her eyes blurry. There was something there.

Hope blinked, trying to focus, but there was something blue floating in the sea. She stopped, rubbed her eyes and stared down again, and then there was something closer to white.

Hope abruptly livened up, and ran back along the path until she found the steps down to the beach. The tide seemed to make its way up to the beach where there was a slight cove, and she wondered if things funnelled into here. As she got closer, she noticed the item was a blue cloth that seemed to have floated in and was now being deposited on the beach. She reached forward into the sea, realizing that it was a tartan.

Hope managed to secure one hand onto the cloth and pulled the heavy garment out of the water. As it lay on the beach, she recognised it for the tartan her aunt always wore. She spread it out and knew the shawl before her. Hope's eyes watered again, realising the pain in her heart was now being backed up with evidence. For a moment she shivered, looked out to sea again, but her eyes saw something else.

It was the white thing again. It bobbed to the surface briefly and then descended again. How far out was it? Maybe ten meters, or was it more? Hope was not in a great state. Tears were running down her eyes, but she decided that she should go and retrieve this item as well. It might be something of her aunt's, something else she could keep.

Stepping into the water, Hope kept going as it passed her knees. Her jeans became soaked, the boots she was wearing filling up, and she felt the cold around her feet. Hope continued until the water soon passed her waist and was now rising above her chest. The item was floating away and she watched as it began to sink. Now the water was at her shoulders and Hope's hair, buffeted by the wind, began to sit heavier as the ends of it touched the sea.

Well, she was this far out, she might as well try and see. Hope was a strong swimmer and always had been, even saving a few lives due to her expertise at the art, but she would have to be careful. This was the sea in all its elements and if she wasn't careful, she might not make it back.

Hope ducked under the water, began to pull herself forward, peering into the dark sea. At first, she couldn't see anything, but then she thought she caught a flash of white over to the left-hand side. Hope swam over, finding something in front of her. She reached out carefully, her view blurred by the water, but her hand touched something else.

A chill went down Hope's spine, and she struggled not to panic. Her hand had engaged another hand. Her first instinct was to recoil, but she'd gone for this item, so she reached forward, touching it and found herself in a handshake. She kicked backwards, struggling to find her way back to shore until she broke the surface. She looked around to try and make sure she was going the correct direction.

Hope kicked hard with her feet, pulling herself along with her free hand, but her other hand remained clenched to the appendage she'd grabbed. Finally, her feet touched sand and as she hauled herself along, the water started to descend below her shoulders. She didn't look back at what she was dragging, rather just kept going, feeling the appendage get more and more heavy as the water got shallower. Eventually, it was pulling her shoulder back and down as she dragged it along the sand.

Once clear of where the surf was arriving, Hope let go and collapsed, spluttering, into the sand. She turned back and looked, seeing before her a single arm with an open hand at the end. The arm was bare but as she looked at the rear of the hand, she saw a ring on the middle finger. She was not au fait with every piece of her aunt's jewellery, but she was with that one. The ring had come from a man she had met in Congo back in the sixties; a man she had talked about as being the one man she might have loved for life, and now here in death, the ring was still on the finger.

Chapter 2

Detective Inspector Seoras Macleod was having a busy day at the office. There was a large amount of paperwork to tidy up, something he didn't enjoy. Usually, Hope would make sure everything was sorted, and with the assistance of DC Ross, the paperwork was meticulously filed. But Hope had disappeared off to the Isle of Eigg because of her deceased auntie. Now Macleod was having to pick up the load.

His other sergeant, Clarissa Urquhart had cunningly required to go for a medical that day which Macleod was convinced she had done deliberately. She'd seemed fine all week but suddenly there was a problem with the back of her thigh. She couldn't walk correctly. There were issues there and she needed to get it checked out. As there was no ongoing case, he could hardly refuse, but he was sure that Clarissa had smirked when she left his office. In truth, Macleod was just faffing, for Ross was picking up most of the paperwork. In true fashion, he would have it pristine and neat by the end of the day.

Macleod wondered, was this what Hope did? Simply take

everything from Macleod and dump it on Ross? Was that not how the wheels of life work?

Macleod was also worried. He hadn't seen Hope seem so downhearted since her aunt died. At first, in front of everyone, she had regaled them with tales of her aunt, saying that all the light was now gone from life. Hope was okay and was just blessed by having such a person for so long. But Macleod had not seen so many bereaved people in his life not to be able to spot others who were lying, maybe not intentionally, but certainly to themselves. When he'd asked Jane what he should do for Hope, his life partner had simply looked at him before announcing he should be there for her. How would he be there for Hope?

He would have to wait for those moments. Anyway, she had a new man in her life; she didn't need some crusty boss to put an arm around her anymore. Her partner, the Car-Hire-Man, as he'd become affectionately known in the office, was seemingly good for her. Yet Macleod had seen Hope's face, the day she left the office before travelling down to Oban, and he could tell the pain behind the eyes.

Macleod sat down and looked at the pages in front of him. Ross had said simply, 'Check it over. Just make sure it's all right.' Macleod thought he should leave it. He put most of the words together that were on the paper in front of him. It was just that he couldn't be bothered reading them again. Most of the deaths he was reporting on had been mundane, murder not part of it. It was one of those things that they had to go and check. Sometimes things look suspicious even when they really weren't.

Macleod's phone rang and in a movement that would possibly give him a sore shoulder for the rest of the day, he instantly whipped his arm out and picked it up.

'Macleod.'

'Seoras, it's Hope. I'm going to need someone.'

That was quite an admission for Hope to say that. Macleod thought of the best words to say. 'Okay,' was all that he managed.

'Not like that, Seoras. It's about Mary. I've found her. Well, I've found a bit of her.'

'What?' Macleod started. 'How do you mean you've found part of her?'

'Out in the sea. I spotted something in the sea. It's part of her. It's her arm, Seoras. Just her arm.'

'How do you know it's her arm?' Macleod nearly cursed at himself, for that was so like a detective. This was not just an arm that they'd come across in an investigation. This was Hope's aunt and he needed to be more tactful. Sometimes it was easier with suspects, but the pair of them had seen so many bodies together. There was almost a dark humour that surrounded it. Certainly, an abruptness that would not be deemed polite to those who had suffered.

'The ring on her finger, it's hers. I need someone. It just seems a bit strange. Why is her arm here?'

'It's been out in the sea, Hope,' said Macleod. 'I wouldn't read too much into it. How did she die?'

'They said she fell off the cliff path.'

'Well, she could have lost it in the fall.'

'I don't like it, Seoras. I'm not sure that that's what happened. It just doesn't feel right. I've got her shawl with it as well. The arm's also bare.'

'Well, if your aunt was wearing a shawl, what would she have worn underneath it?' asked Macleod.

10

'She was eighty-one, Seoras. She was aging well but the weather was inclement. She didn't go to skinny dip.'

'No, I understand that,' said Macleod, trying his best not to sound flippant. 'What would she have been wearing?'

'Well, she'd have worn a blouse or a jumper or something. Very strange the arm doesn't have it on it.'

'If it got lost in the fall,' said Macleod, 'it could happen. I tell you what, I'm going to send Jona down.'

Jona Nakamura was the station senior forensic officer but was also the housemate of Hope McGrath, although Hope was spending more time at the flat of Car-Hire-Man than she was at her own home these days.

'Sounds like you need someone and Jona's got the skills and abilities to put your mind at rest about what happened to your aunt. I could come down and have a look, but I haven't got that.'

'I wasn't suggesting you come,' said Hope. 'It's just something's not right.'

'Okay,' said Macleod. 'I'll get hold of Jona, get her down soon as. We'll get to the bottom of this, okay? Are you all right?'

'I don't know, Seoras. She's just gone. It's weird coming here. I haven't seen her for a year, but I still expect her to turn up. I was in her room and there's all the photographs of me as a child, me when I became a sergeant. She was prouder than you the day I became a sergeant.'

Macleod let the comment go because he'd always tried to be detached regarding the promotion of his colleagues. But he had been proud. He'd seen Hope grow and she was still growing, hopefully into an officer as good as he was. Macleod had no conceit when he said that. He knew what he was. Maybe a ham-fisted friend, maybe someone who struggled with today's politics and his attitude around women, but the one thing he was, was a good detective.

'And she'd have every right to be proud,' said Macleod. And he thought of his partner, Jane, who surely would've beamed at that comment. He had pitched it right.

'I'll await Jona but let me go and talk to some other people, see what I can dig up.'

'Don't,' said Macleod, suddenly switching into his inspector mode.

'Why?' asked Hope.

'You're emotionally attached to your aunt. You are attached by blood. The last thing we need is for you to go asking questions and even putting in an accusation at a time when we don't know if anything untoward has happened. You're also not yourself at the moment,' said Macleod, wanting better words. 'If it comes to it and Jona does find something that's untoward, I will come, and we'll investigate it together. But I don't trust you at this point, Hope. As good a detective as you are, I don't trust you when it's such a close family connection.'

'I've been a detective for a while now, sir,' said Hope. 'I think I can handle it.'

'Don't take this the wrong way, Hope. I wouldn't trust myself. Go back to her room, look around her room, look around anywhere she's been, but do not begin any sort of investigation. Am I clear?'

'Yes, yes, Seoras. You're probably right. Sorry.'

'There's no need to apologise. You're just in a heck of a situation. I'll have Jona come down soon as. But it'll probably be the morning before she gets there, I would think.'

'It'll give me time to walk around and think,' said Hope. 'I'll see her tomorrow.'

'Good,' said Macleod, 'Do that. Take time to heal.'

When Macleod came off the phone, he thought about picking it up again and calling Jona, but instead, he stood up and made his way across the station to the forensic offices. This needed to be dealt with sympathetically, and so required to be delivered first-hand. He couldn't think of a better person to deal with the circumstance than the diminutive Asian woman.

* * *

Jona Nakamura looked around the room and saw the photographs of Hope. She'd arrived that morning on the ferry and had gone straight with Hope up to the Singing Sands Later but Better Township and to the room of Mary McGrath. Hope had insisted it had been locked for she'd left the arm in there, wrapped up tight and placed it inside the fridge. Jona smiled, looking around the room.

'She certainly liked you, didn't she?' said Jona.

Hope grinned. 'She was my biggest advocate. When I had doubts, she'd tell me I could do it. More so than Macleod. The Inspector chivvies you along, but he's a teacher. He's a mentor. My aunt was my supporter. That's what I realise now. Even though I rarely saw her, every time I spoke to her, she was the one boosting me, telling me I can do this.'

'Well, she wasn't wrong,' said Jona. 'Is that the fridge over there?'

Hope nodded. Jona made her way to the fridge, opened the door, and took out a bundled-up package. Making her way over to a table in the middle of the room, Jona placed the package down. Snapping on her forensic gloves, Jona

13

unwrapped it slowly and saw the white flesh underneath. It was bloated, having been in the water for a while. She carefully bent down and started to examine it.

Hope looked the other way. It was funny that she had to do this given she had looked at many a corpse in her time, but those corpses had not been family.

'And you identified her from the ring? I take it there's no tattoos or other markings on the arm?'

'Wrong arm,' said Hope. 'She had her tattoos on the other arm. One she got in Bangkok. Don't even ask me how she got that one. I think that was a wild night with I don't know who.' Hope raised her eyes and Jona gave a chuckle.

'Well, the arm's certainly been in the water for two to three weeks, but you could probably tell that yourself,' said Jona. 'It's lost a lot of blood but again, it's been in the water, and you would expect if it was severed, that that would happen. But—' There was a silence as Jona leaned in, looking at the end of the arm.

'But what?' asked Hope. 'Something wrong?'

Jona stood up, made her way over to a small bag she had, and took out a couple of small implements. 'Just a moment,' she said. 'I don't want to say anything until . . . I just need a better look.' Jona returned to the table and started poking at the end of the arm.

'What are you doing?' asked Hope.

'Shush,' said Jona. 'I'm working. I need to have a look at this.'

Hope felt her feet beginning to tap and instead turned and walked along the room to the far end and looked out of the window. The wind was still whipping along strongly and a drizzle was beginning. The view from the window was spectacular. If there had been any heat or sunlight, Hope

14

would've gone out on the balcony and sat down. But today, she'd have found it quite cold.

'You know, Seoras sent you down because he thought you'd be the best company for me. He values you a lot, Jona. The clever one. The counsellor. The one that's able to talk to people. He probably thinks you're going to be doing a shrink job on me. Help me out. What I need is somebody to sit down and have a few beers with.'

'You might want to sit down for this,' said Jona. 'There might be a shrink job after all.'

'Why? What's the big deal?' said Hope.

'This arm. If you look at the end of it—When I saw it at first, I thought yes, but I thought I'd better not say until I was one hundred percent sure.'

'Sure of what?' asked Hope. 'What are you trying to tell me?'

'Hope, you'd better ring Macleod, get him down here. That arm's been severed.'

'Yes, it's come off, probably when she fell,' said Hope.

'No,' said Jona, shaking her head emphatically. 'It's been cut off.'

Chapter 3

'Clarissa, can you come in a minute?'

Macleod waved at his sergeant from the door but saw DC Ross flicking his head up from his desk. 'In fact, Ross, join us as well.'

Clarissa Urquhart, a sergeant in the unit, rolled her eyes at Ross, and together, the two of them stood up and made their way to Macleod's office. As they entered, they went to sit down at the conference desk in the corner but Macleod was still behind his own main desk, and instead, pointed to two seats in front of him.

'Plonk yourselves down there quickly.' The Inspector seemed agitated. 'I'm on the road in about twenty minutes. I'm just waiting for Jane to come in with some of my bags, and I might be gone a couple of days.'

'Trouble at home?' asked Clarissa. Macleod raised an eyebrow as if she'd dare ask.

'No, Sergeant. Jane is simply bringing me some clothing because I need to go down to Hope. I'll be on the Isle of Eigg, Ross, but both of you keep a good contact.'

'Is she all right?' asked Ross.

'No. Jona is already down there, and it appears that we may have a case developing.'

'I can cover it for if you want, Inspector.'

'No,' said Macleod. 'You both know that Hope was off to visit the grave of her aunt. Well, what was left behind. Her aunt disappeared from the Isle of Eigg, thought swept out to sea, but when she was down there, Hope saw something in the water and retrieved an arm and a shawl. The shawl belonged to her aunt. I sent Jona down, and she believes the arm also belongs to her aunt.'

'Blimey,' said Ross. 'Is Hope okay?'

'I'll tell you when I'm down there,' said Macleod. 'To be frank, I'd be surprised if she is. That's why I sent Jona down. Well, one of two reasons. The other was Jona's checked the arm and it appears it was cut from the body, not torn by the sea, or rocks, or any fall.'

'Are you sure you don't want all of us?' asked Clarissa with a much more serious face on.

'No,' said Macleod. 'I want you both here. I've found over my time that these island jobs don't tend to stay on the island. We need to go looking at histories of people and that quite often happens on the mainland. And I also need someone to man the fort while I'm away. You've got enough experience, Clarissa. Just don't cheese anybody off when you're doing it.'

Clarissa took the pink scarf she was wearing and flung it around her neck almost indignantly. 'I have absolutely no idea what you mean.'

Macleod lowered his eyes at her. His lips pursed in tightly. 'Try and be like Ross, polite to everyone.'

'I wouldn't say I'm like that, sir.'

'You are, Ross, and it's a good thing, so enough. Anyway, Jane

17

will be here in a minute. Ross, file the rest of that paperwork we were doing. Clarissa, take care of things here. Anything minor, take a first look at it and I'll be in touch with anything I need. Eigg's not in the middle of nowhere. I will be contactable.'

'Have you seen the weather closing in? Are you going to get on the ferry?' asked Clarissa.

'That's why I'm going now. I need to get down and get over. It might be a day or two without the ferry from the looks of it.'

'What was her aunt doing on Eigg anyway?' asked Ross.

'New retirement home. Well, sort of a township special thing. I think she was quite eccentric, but I'll have more when I'm down.'

'Are you driving down?' asked Clarissa.

'Yes. What's wrong with that?' asked Macleod.

'You don't do much of that normally. Just wondering. Thought you might get one of the uniforms to drive you down.'

'I'm not going to tie up police resources for no reason,' said Macleod, and then clocked the cheeky smile on Clarissa's face. 'That's enough, Sergeant. Hope might actually need me down there. I can do without that. Dismissed.'

Clarissa got up with a grin on her face and refused Ross's invitation to exit the room first, instead lingering until the man had left the room.

'Don't worry, Seoras, I've got this. I can be a bit brash with people, but I'm not an ass. And give her our best. She's got to be hurting.'

'That she is.'

* * *

Hope wandered into the common lounge of the retirement

18

home. While each resident had a rather spacious room come house, there was also a central welcoming area complete with sofas, suites, and little breakout areas where they could go and talk to relatives or anyone else on their own, but Hope noticed that today it was distinctly quiet. She wondered how many visitors anyone got here, but also noted that there were a couple of spare rooms at the residents' disposal.

Hope sat down on the seat in front of a large window looking out towards the sea. The previous night, she had walked a long distance across the island, keeping away from anyone as she thought about her aunt, but this morning she'd woken with a new drive and was itching to get on with an investigation. Macleod would be over on the first ferry, having motored down the previous evening. His call from Oban was appreciated, but she'd cut him off quickly, wanting to keep to her own thoughts. Now she sat in the common lounge awaiting his arrival. It'd be a few hours and she just simply wanted to get on with investigating—anything else to fill her mind rather than sitting and thinking about her aunt, especially about her untimely ending.

'Hello, dear. Are you looking for someone?'

'Sorry,' said Hope, looking over at a woman with grey hair. It was tightly held around her head, probably with a large dose of lacquer, as Aunt Mary would have called it, but the woman had a pleasant smile. She had lived life, that was obvious from the various wrinkles across her face, but it was a kind face and she smiled delicately, although looking at her teeth, Hope swore they must have been dentures. No one's teeth could be that perfect at this stage of life. Ever the detective, she thought to herself, noticing the detailing when people are just trying to be nice to you.

'Sorry,' said Hope. 'I'm Mary McGrath's niece. I just came down to look over her things and that.'

'Oh, sweet Mary. She was quite a one.' Hope recognised the American accent in the voice of the woman but that was as far as she could place it. Where in America? Who knew? 'Such a tragedy. She was a lovely woman too. Always on the go. Made me laugh.'

'That she did with people,' said Hope. 'Sorry, but who are you?'

'Oh, apologies. My name is Nancy. Nancy Griffin.'

'Nice to meet you, Nancy. You're American by the sounds of it.'

'Alaska. Well, a long time ago. America hasn't been home for the best part of forty years. Been out and about around the world and that. Did I say forty? Oh, no. It was maybe forty, twenty years ago. That's the trouble with time. It just passes. You do well to be busy, then you don't notice it. Do you know? I still feel like I'm fifty.'

Hope sized the woman up, reckoning that she was reasonably fit for her years. Surely, she was in her eighties. She was wearing a pair of pink slippers, purple slacks and a white jumper, and Hope smiled as the woman made her way over and sat down beside her. Her movements were graceful and Hope wondered, did she have any particular ailments that one would expect at that time of life? Was it the cod liver oil that everybody had? Is that what kept her moving so easily?

'You're looking well for your age,' said Hope.

'Thank you, dear. I do all right, you know. I get about. Not like your aunt this last wee while. She was struggling with that hip.'

'Her hip?' queried Hope. This was the first she'd heard about any hip injury. 'What was wrong with her?'

'Oh, nothing in particular. Just one of those things you get. She fell and the hip was giving her trouble. I mean, seemed a bit crazy what happened to her, considering.'

Hope stared into the old woman's face and saw a look in her eye that was almost mischievous.

'What do you mean by that?'

'Well, several weeks before that she couldn't make it over to the path. Then one night she disappears. Just goes out there. I can understand that if something happened she would struggle to recover but I can't believe she was out there.'

'That's what the home said. The manager said that they'd seen her go out.'

'Well, I didn't see her go out. Not many of the other residents did either.'

'She said she probably went out towards the sands. Said she loved them.'

'They're not wrong with that. There's certainly a half-truth there. As far as I recall, your aunt always loved that sort of thing.'

Hope wondered if the woman was all right. Her aunt had only been there less than a year. She hadn't been there long enough for people to reminisce. Or maybe the days just seemed to be like that now that they were all together, so far away from anywhere else. But the woman seemed fluid otherwise. Or was it the mind that was playing tricks with her?

'How long have you known my aunt?'

The woman looked off out of the window as if recalling something from the past. 'Just since I got here,' she said. 'Feels like a lifetime though when you get someone you like. My husband liked her too. Had to be careful though. I think she turned his head.' The woman laughed briefly, but it felt rather forced.

'Do you like it here?' asked Hope.

'It's perfect. It's just a pity we've lost so many people. Three of them.'

'What happened to the other two?' asked Hope. 'I saw the graves.'

'They're not graves. They're just where a couple of empty caskets are. Your aunt's out with them. Out there under the sea, enjoying themselves.'

'What, they fell off the path as well?' asked Hope.

'No, no, no. No, I reckon things just got too much for John. Reckon he jumped. He was always a morbid fellow, was John, and Natalie, well, we're not sure what happened to Natalie. Was out that way though. It's dangerous around here, the sea. They told us that when we bought the brochure. We had a look. It is beautiful, but it's wild. You got to be careful when things are wild. Got to look after yourself. That's the one thing we've always done was looked after ourselves. Whatever the cost. Look after yourself.'

The woman seemed to be drifting away somewhere else and rather than interrupt her, Hope sat calmly.

With a jolt, the woman returned. 'But where's my manners? Can I get you anything? I mean, you are the niece of Mary McGrath. You're the policewoman, aren't you?'

'That's right, I'm Detective Sergeant Hope McGrath.'

'I recognise you from all the photographs in her room. Proud as punch of you. Proud as punch. She always held a light out for you. That's what your aunt always said. There's always Hope. It's sad that you missed her. I thought you were going to be coming down before this.'

'It's been a bit busy at work. I never got the chance. We spoke a lot on the phone, and she was wanting me down, but she never would have imposed.'

'No, she wouldn't,' said Nancy. 'That wasn't Mary's way. Sometimes you think she'd have been better by imposing. Been better to just put her foot down.'

Again, the woman seemed to be disappearing, off somewhere else, and Hope wondered whether she was really okay.

'There you are,' said a voice from behind and Hope turned to see an elderly man making his way over. If Nancy looked well for her years, the man looked quite the opposite, although that may have been due to the fact that his hair, as thin as it was, was looking extremely distressed. He was in a dressing gown and from what Hope could tell didn't have much on underneath.

'Nancy, where's that talcum powder?'

Nancy snapped back from wherever she was. 'Oh, bottom cupboard.'

'Why'd you put it in the bottom cupboard? That's not your cupboard.'

'And it's not my talcum powder, it's yours. It's your cupboard at the bottom, that's why I put it in there.'

'We said the talcum powder was yours. I'm only borrowing it.'

'No, we didn't. Anyway, Jake, this is Mary McGrath's niece. This is Hope.'

Hope thought she said it like she was some sort of expected Messiah they'd been waiting for, but all she could think to do was to hold up her hand and say hi.

'Oh, Mary's niece. Stand up then,' said Jake. Hope found herself standing up. 'Turn around.'

'Is that really necessary, Jake?'

'Well, she talked about her all the time. She said she's six foot, she's gorgeous, and she'll break the heart of many a man.'

'And if she has anything like her auntie's charm, she'll do it too,' said Nancy.

'My, my, she wasn't wrong, your aunt, was she? I bet you knock 'em dead.'

'You can't say that these days,' said Nancy.

'Ah, don't mind me, love. I'm just a daft old fool. Back in my day, you could tell a woman how good she looked, and she didn't take any offense at it either. Mary said you're smart as you are good-looking. If you're anywhere half as near that, you'll be a quite clever cookie.'

'Jake, just get back and get your talcum powder on,' said Nancy,

'Oh, right, will do. You're right. I have nothing on under this. Whoops.' And with that, Jake left abruptly, heading back to one of the doors at the far end of the complex.

'I apologise for my husband. He's very forward, very engaging, and he means nothing about getting you to stand up; that's just his daft way. He's very gentle.'

'I'm sure he is,' said Hope.

'But I'd best go and see he's all right. He gets a little absent-minded. He's not daft. Just the mind's got the odd gap. You'll get it too, love, when it comes. Hope you don't get it too bad. Anyway, it's lovely to meet you. Will you be here for long?'

'I might be around for a while,' said Hope.

'Good. It'll be nice having you here with Mary gone. I miss her.' And with that, Nancy stood up and left. Hope looked down at her watch. Macleod should be in in a couple of hours. Maybe she'd take a walk around the island before meeting

24

him down at the ferry. Jona had asked not to be disturbed because she had plenty of work still to do from Inverness that was being sent down to her. But she was also getting the arm ready, to ship back up. *Yes*, thought Hope, *let's go meet Seoras*.

Chapter 4

Macleod drove off the ferry to find only simple roads ahead of him. The island was sparsely populated, and his was one of only two cars that had come off the ferry that morning. His night in Oban had been one of fitful sleep, which he put down to worrying about his sergeant, and he was delighted to see her across the road as he came off the ferry. Driving over, he pulled up alongside and watched as Hope opened the door and stepped inside the car. Normally, there was a formality between the two and as closely as they worked, they were still officers, colleagues as much as friends; but Hope leaned over, threw her arms around Macleod and buried her face on his shoulder. He felt her beginning to weep and rather than move, simply put his arms around her too, holding her tight into him. After about a minute, Hope straightened up, and started drying her eyes.

'Sorry, Seoras. It's just I haven't had someone to sit down with like that. Someone to just collapse on.'

'I sent you Jona; was she no help?'

'Jona's lovely but then she got involved in all the forensic work and she's off and running. I needed someone to just stop.

Someone to just be a shoulder.'

'I'm here now,' said Macleod, 'and if needs be, you can have this shoulder anytime, but I intend to get to the bottom of this. Are you okay to come along on the interviews?'

'I'm not sure. I was talking to some of the residents earlier on.'

'What did I say about not investigating?'

'I wasn't, Seoras, I wasn't. I was sitting looking out the window and a woman came along. Nancy. Nancy and Jake. Americans. Nice people, but he did come out in just his dressing gown. I think he's a little bit forgetful.'

'Okay. You seem quite shaken, Hope. I tell you what, I'm going to go up and see the manager at the home, and I'll start there. Once I come out from her and we start to talk to the residents, then you can join me.'

'Why?' asked Hope.

'Let's say we need to be careful. This is your aunt who's passed on. However she got out there, if there's any issue with what the home's done, that can impact you quite strongly. I don't want my sergeant sitting there having a go at people. You seem very raw over this, and that's fine. I expect that, but I'll start off.'

'If you think that's wise, Seoras.'

Macleod nodded and drove the car across the island of Eigg, taking in the dynamic scenery. The sheer amount of grass and little hidden away houses with so few neighbours around them struck him. His own house in the Black Isle on Inverness was hidden away behind trees and looked out onto the Moray Firth, but from this island, if you looked west, you saw so much sea, with a view of the mainland looking back over your shoulder.

As he took the road out towards the retirement home, he realised just how good the road was compared to the others on the island. There was a stark change from that of the home to that of the normal public roads. He parked in a small but immaculately kept car park. Stepping out of the car, Macleod felt the wind around his legs and reached into the back for his long coat. Suitably wrapped up, he nodded at Hope to accompany him. 'Can't have you sitting in the car,' he said. 'I'm sure there'll be somewhere for you to sit.'

'There's a day lounge I was in before, Seoras. I'll go sit there. They're quite good with the coffee and stuff, you know. They do look after you.' Macleod nodded, and when he entered through a set of large double doors, he found a bell to ring on his left-hand side. There was no receptionist, for after all, this was a home, albeit a retirement home.

Soon a young woman appeared before him, dressed in a smart pair of black slacks and a cream blouse. A pair of glasses, wide-rimmed, give her the appearance of someone with binoculars on her face, and her brown hair barely touched her shoulders. 'You must be the inspector. I'm Janey Smart, the manager. I've briefly met your colleague before. Are you okay?' The woman looked at Hope.

'It's taking time to sink in, but you've been very hospitable, as have some of the residents.'

'Well, we do what we can to help. I guess you'll want somewhere more formal for us to chat,' said Janey. 'If you wish you can come into my office, Inspector.'

'Thank you,' said Macleod and pulled out his credentials, holding them up in front of the manager.

'Oh, there's no need for that. I hardly think that someone's going to come over here pretending to be an inspector.'

'You should always take care, Miss Smart, but I am glad you feel at ease.' With that Macleod followed the woman down a short corridor.

'Is your colleague not coming with you?'

'No, I think it's a wee bit close to the bone at the moment. I think it best if you and I have a word, Miss Smart.'

'Please, Janey. There's no need to be so formal. We're not that way here at all. I am the manager, but I try and sort of fit in with the residents. I do live here.'

'You have a room on site?'

'Not a room, Inspector. I have a small house out the back. It's detached, it's away from the residents, and not with quite the views they have. It's efficient for me. Although if I ever have a family one day, I'd probably move further on into the island. Find somewhere there.'

'Okay,' said Macleod. 'Did that come with the job?'

'It came with the building, because I decided that and we built it. My father built this place. It comes out of our business. I mean, this is how I make my money.'

She opened a door and ushered Macleod into an office, pointing to a corner where a small table was located. 'Coffee, Inspector?'

'Black, please,' said Macleod. 'Thank you.' Janey made her way across the office to where Macleod saw a cafetière and a kettle. The woman started to boil the kettle and pour some ground coffee into the cafetière.

'Do you like your coffee, Inspector?'

'Always,' said Macleod.

'I find it helps me work. There's an American couple here. They seem to drink Java all the time. I can't get with it, far too bitter. This is Kenyan.'

29

'I'm sure it'll be absolutely fine,' said Macleod, but his particular favourite came from Nicaragua, though he wouldn't be rude enough to point that out. 'You say that this is your income. How does that work exactly?'

Janey turned around, lifted herself up onto the sideboard the cafetière was sitting on. Sitting there, she began to swing her legs back and forward like a schoolgirl.

'This is my father's gift to me. He had this dream about building a home like this, and when he came to Eigg, he fell in love with it. It took a while to get it through with the community, but we built it and then had to go and look for residents. You don't just pitch up here and decide to buy the place. We were looking for people of a particular type. It can be right rough here in the winter, but everything's spectacular. This is not a cosy care home. We called it a retirement township. A place where there's assistance but generally, you're left to get on with it. Everything also of the highest standard. It was a certain pitch we were doing, and thankfully, plenty bought into it. The idea is that you come here and you're here to stay. We even have a graveyard up the road. That's where they are buried, the three we've lost so far.'

'I thought they were lost out to sea.'

'Yes, but we do bury a casket. We have a funeral of sorts. I think it's just easier, isn't it? Once you know they're dead.'

'And are you certain they're dead?' asked Macleod. 'Lost to sea. Nobody actually saw them go in, did they?'

'That's correct, but they were out there, and they never left on the ferry. Unless they had their own submarine or a helicopter coming to pick them up, I don't think they left the island, Inspector, I'm sad to say.' With that, she jumped down, hearing the kettle click, and poured the water into the cafetière. She brought it over with two cups, placed one in front of Macleod. 'We tend to get the adventurous type here.'

'Still, it's a strange location,' said Macleod. 'Not a lot of facilities.'

'On the contrary, Inspector, when we built this place, we built a gym. There's a small pool as well. We have people coming up from the island too, hairdressers, massage people, counsellors. You can get everything you want. We made sure of that. We have a chef who does fine dining if the residents want it, and quite often, the residents do eat together. It's like their small restaurant. We are exclusive.'

'Even so,' said Macleod, 'but why here?'

'The sands, Inspector. If you go to the sands and you walk on them, they sing to you.' The woman beamed as if she was telling a fairy tale to a child.

'Sing? How on earth does sand sing to you?'

'It's to do with the silica, but you can hear singing when you walk across it. It's quite intoxicating, entrancing. I sometimes wonder is that what happened to Joel and Natalie? We don't quite know where they went from. Mary, too. Although we think Mary was up on the path and fell off.'

'Why do you think that?' asked Macleod.

'We have a book. When you leave to go out somewhere, you just sign the book to say you're out. It's more a precaution so if we have a fire drill or if something happens, we know we're not looking for you in the building. A fairly standard idea.'

Macleod nodded. 'That sounds sensible, but why do you think she was on the path?'

'Because that's where Mary went, and she loved to look down. Especially that last week, I'm not sure she was feeling that great. It's quite a walk down to the sand, but you can view

31

much more from up above.'

'Is the path safe?' asked Macleod. 'I mean for people of their years.'

'I think you'll find here, they don't like you to say people of their age. Most of the people here are certainly not infirm. Mary had a slight issue with her hip the last weeks before she died. I think that would've kept her from going down onto the sand.'

Janey poured the coffee. Macleod took a drink, chewing the coffee around his mouth.

'Ah, a man that actually drinks coffee, enjoys coffee, and doesn't treat it as an optional extra for his work.'

Macleod raised his eyes slowly. The woman was like an excited schoolgirl, and it felt wrong. He was the police, and there were three people dead. He was coming to look to see if there was anything unusual in the deaths. Most managers would've been apprehensive. 'How long after they went missing,' asked Macleod, 'did you get search parties going?'

'Within a few hours. We had lifeboats out as well, but no one was ever found. You can check with the Coastguard.'

'Basically,' said Macleod, 'your residents went out for a walk on their own and didn't come back.'

'You put it that coldly, but it is accurate,' said Janey. 'Sad, but you can see why we presume they're dead. That's why we had these funerals, albeit with nothing to bury. Gives the rest of the residents closure. They get to know each other very well. It's like living on a street. I tend not to bother them. Let them get on with their little lives, make sure that everything's here, provide for them. I take care of the business side of things. They're paying their rent; I sort out the bank. I take my salary and I'm here for the next ten years at least, if not more. It's what my father did for me.'

'Did for you? Did you have a previous job?' asked Macleod. The woman stood up and almost skipped across to a filing cabinet before she pulled open the bottom drawer and reached inside. Making her way back across, she threw a photograph in front of Macleod, and he saw a woman standing there, dressed in white with a tennis racket.

'I was going to be a superstar. I actually competed in a number of tournaments. I did all right, but nothing like getting up to the top. The man beside me there is my coach. He's from Bulgaria. Basically, he took my father and me for a ride. He was charging things against our name left, right, and centre, which kept stringing it out. What really got it in the end was he made a pass at me, and my father pulled me out of the system completely. He was right. I was never good enough to make it as a tennis player, didn't have enough about me. But Gregor, he kept saying I did, kept pushing for more, and Father poured more and more money in. When he pulled me out, I didn't really have a lot of qualifications. This is what Father does. He builds stuff, you know?'

'Builds stuff? In what way?' asked Macleod.

'Homes, houses, grand schemes. He's not just an architect. He's got his own business behind it. He came up with this brainchild, that he was going to be running anyway, and he needed somebody to be here for it. And I needed time away from everything. Time to have something simple to look after and plenty of rest time to do a bit of work and study, get myself back on track. He's turning me into a manager.' The photograph was whisked away from underneath Macleod and put back in the bottom drawer.

'I think I'm going to have to go and talk to your residents. I have to inform you, there's quite a bit of suspicion around the body of Mary McGrath. That's why I'm here.'

'Suspicion? But she fell off the path, surely.'

'That's not strictly true, although it may have contributed. Possibly she was pushed. Possibly she was never up there. From what little you can tell me, all I know is that Mary went out. And from what my forensic officer can tell me, somebody took her arm off.'

Macleod saw the woman's shocked face. 'What do you mean, took her arm off?'

'The arm that my sergeant found in the sea had been cut off. Not ripped, not torn, cut.'

'Like with a knife?'

'I'm not sure of the implement. My forensic officer's still working on it, but something of that ilk.'

Janey sat down in the seat opposite Macleod. 'Blimey. But you think somebody—?'

'I don't think,' said Macleod. 'When somebody gets their arm cut off like that, there is a large degree of suspicion that murder is involved.'

Chapter 5

While Macleod was engaged with the manager of the township, Hope sat in the luxurious day room, looking out to the sea to the west of Eigg. She felt anxious, and anger was brewing up inside her. Since Jona had said that her aunt's arm had been cut off, Hope had been struggling with the concept that someone had murdered her here in a retirement home, the place she'd chosen to live out her last days. Hope couldn't grasp that her Aunt's days would've ended so soon.

If the elements had taken her, that would've been okay because that's how Mary lived. Her life was out there on the edge, running around here and there, but for somebody to have stopped her was heartbreaking. She would have to wait for Macleod. He was right in thinking that she was too close to this case. He would have to take the lead, manage it, make sure it was done professionally. Although something she prided herself on, she wasn't sure she could keep a prudent distance between the investigation and her love for her aunt.

There was the sound of footsteps entering the room, and Hope turned to see a tall, elegant man, complete with a Panama hat. To look at him you'd have thought outside was the perfect day for English cricket, rather than a rapidly deteriorating Scottish morning. He had that home-counties feel. The long legs with the clean slacks, the shirt with a small cravat, and a gentle if somewhat guarded smile.

'Excuse me, my dear, are you looking for someone?'

'No,' said Hope, 'I'm waiting. My boss is just in speaking to your manager.'

'Oh, right, is that something to do with the toilets?'

Hope stifled a giggle. 'No, it's nothing to do with the toilets. I'm Mary McGrath's niece.'

The man stepped over quickly, his hands out. 'Oh, well, God love you, such a terrible thing to have happened to her. Please, sit down, sit down. I'm Daniel, Daniel Edwards. I was just taking a quick walk before going back. The cricket's on from India. Some of our boys are in it. I like my cricket, but sorry, you're Mary's niece?'

'Yes,' said Hope, 'Mary's niece. Did you know her well?'

'We all know each other well here. It's quite homely as you can see. Yes, it's billed as independent living, but we do tend to get along together, tend to share a lot of things. We have a chef—you can sit and eat together in the evenings, which is rather nice considering the fact that there's not that many of us. We do tend to use him quite a bit, so I guess it's worthwhile. Well, certainly worthwhile the money we pay them.'

'I take it it's quite an expensive place to live,' said Hope. 'I am aware that Mary had quite a lot of money behind her. Quite successful with her books, writing about her travels.'

'She did, didn't she? She had quite a lot of travels. I've read most of them,' said Daniel. 'I made my money, part of a tea business, hence the India connection. Saw a lot of cricket out there as well. Not done bad for itself as a country, has it?

Considering what they started with. People talk a lot about our empire, I don't know, were we good? Were we bad for it?'

The man stared at Hope, waiting for an answer, which she felt unable to give.

'I haven't really thought about it that much.'

'Oh, sorry, of course, you're here about Mary. You obviously haven't been before. Did they take you up to the grave?'

'I saw it on the way around earlier on, and where they say she went in.'

'Yes, she did go in, although we never found anything of her.'

'I have,' said Hope. 'Didn't the manager tell you?'

'No,' said Daniel. 'Did you find Mary?'

'I found her shawl, the tartan one. I also found her arm.'

'How awful for you?' said Daniel. 'Something like that. That must have given you quite a shock.'

'I'm a detective sergeant. I'm quite used to seeing dead bodies.'

'Yes, but most of them wouldn't have been family members.' Daniel put his hand across, taking hold of Hope's. 'I do hope you're okay. Do take a moment. That's a tough one. Poor old girl is out there in the sea. Not a great end for her, I'm afraid, but we don't get to choose, do we?'

'In my line of work, most people don't get to choose,' said Hope almost without thinking.

'Indeed,' said Daniel. 'I can only imagine.' There were more footsteps behind her, and Hope looked over to see a man and a woman entering through the front doors of the complex.

'Cricket not on yet, Daniel?'

Daniel stood up and turned, waving over the two people. 'Dennis, Sheila, come, come. This is—well, it's Mary's niece. Did you say your name, love?'

'Hope, Hope McGrath.'

'This is Hope.'

'Of course,' said Sheila, 'you're the girl from the photographs in Mary's room. How awful for you? Are you up to take her stuff?'

'Well actually, I just came up to see where it all happened. I guess I came to say goodbye.'

'You're not going to believe it,' said Daniel, 'but Hope found Mary's shawl, her tartan one.'

'Never had that off her,' said Dennis. 'Not that I thought it was anything particularly noteworthy.'

'It's not the time,' said Sheila giving him a dig in the ribs. 'You have to excuse my husband, we were in the clothing trade. He's got an eye for everything you wear. My dear, you found her?'

'I found her arm,' said Hope. She stood up and she felt like her legs were beginning to shake. She wasn't expecting a group of people. So far, she'd only had to deal with the manager and her own team from the murder squad.

'Positively awful, isn't it?' said Daniel.

Dennis stepped forward, putting his hand out to Hope. He began to shake it.

'My condolences. Lovely woman, lovely woman, Mary. My sincere condolences to you, love. Apologies if at times I sound a little bit rough.'

The man's Glasgow accent shone through, and Hope thought for once she was back on Sauchiehall Street listening to someone rolling out of one of the pubs. Sheila, by contrast, had a more refined Glasgow accent, and Hope wondered how the two of them had got together.

'Thank you. She was quite something. I just don't know

what she was doing out there in this weather.'

'It gets us all,' said Daniel. 'All of us have gone out there and stood and watched; it's intoxicating. We've all got it.'

'Got what, Daniel?' said a voice from the rear. 'What's going on?'

'Oh, Georgie, come on, come on over.' A small woman of around five foot marched over, dressed in a large baggy jumper and blue jeans. She had boots that went all the way up to her knees, which Hope thought was quite unusual for someone in her eighties.

'I was just telling them, Georgie, I was just saying that here the views, they grab you. You can't help but go out and look at them. Can you?'

'That's true, and who's this then?

'Georgie,' said Sheila. 'It's okay, easy; it's Mary's niece.'

'Mary's? Oh, my goodness. You've come up here on your own, love? Take a seat.' Hope found herself being forced back into the seat and Georgie sat beside her. 'I told her she shouldn't go out in that weather. That's the sort of thing that happens.'

'Georgie,' said Daniel. 'You don't need to go on about it. Anyway, she's found something of Mary's.'

'You found something?' said Georgie. 'What?'

'I found her shawl,' said Hope.

'Well, for the love of the wee man, that's something else. Where was it?'

'Out in the sea, I had to just go out and get it, I had to swim.' Hope could feel the memory coming back to her, the cold of the water filling her boots.

'Out in the water? Are you wise? You must be a cracking wee swimmer.'

'I do know how to swim. I am good at it.'

'Mary was a good swimmer too,' said Daniel. 'I always remember that about her, she told me. She used to use the pool though; we rarely went out swimming in the sea here.'

'Auch away with you. She used to go out. Mary liked a quick dip, she said it got the blood going.'

'Yes, but on better days than what we've had. She was using the pool mainly. Every morning she'd be up there.'

'Is that before you got together for your tea and toast?'

'We were just friends having a nice breakfast together.'

'The rest of us don't breakfast together. Do we?' said Georgie. Hope thought she saw a tear in Daniel's eye.

'That's enough, Georgie,' said Daniel. 'Look, she was very special to me, a good friend in these times. A good friend at the end of the days. Look, she's gone now, so let's not be so haphazard with our comments, Georgie. Okay?'

'Well, there's no need to take it like that, but all right, whatever you will. Hope, is that what you said?'

'Yes, it's Hope McGrath.'

'Right. What do you do then?'

'I'm a detective sergeant,' said Hope. 'I work in Inverness in the murder squad.'

'You found her shawl but I guess it wouldn't have affected you that much.'

'Of course, it would affect her, Georgie, for goodness sake.' Daniel at this point was livid, a picture of restraint but with a beast behind his face that was desperate to be unleashed.

'What's going on here? What's this all about?'

Someone else entered the room but Hope couldn't see her until she made her way past everyone and stood in front of her. 'Who's this?'

'This is Mary's niece,' said Daniel.

'Mary's niece,' said the woman. 'Pleased to meet you. It's a terrible hand you've been dealt, terrible hand but it's all God's plan; you have to believe that.'

'We don't have to believe nothing; you're not wise,' said Georgie.

'Can we not go into this?' said Daniel. 'Let's just chill, yes? A bit of refinement, maybe a cup of tea. Sheila?'

'Of course,' said Sheila. 'I take it you'll take a tea.'

Hope shook her head. 'Sorry it's coffee. Is that okay? Just black.'

'Of course, it's fine.'

The new arrival was a greying woman with slightly slumped shoulders. She took Hope by the hand. 'Do you mind if I pray with you?'

'Can I ask your name first?'

'Angusina. My name is Angusina Macleod.'

'You wouldn't be from the Islands, would you?' Hope had recognised Macleod's name and Angusina the female version of Angus, not used these days but previously, a name that was far from uncommon on the Islands.

'I'm from Harris,' she said. 'Well, God has taken me many places in my life, many, many places.' The woman seemed to drift off for a moment, but her hands were firmly clasping Hope's. 'If I can just say a quick word of prayer with you, please.' Before she got an answer, Angusina bowed her head. 'Father, thank you for bringing her here. Thank you for bringing Mary's niece to us. We ask that you will be a boon to her, that you will be with her. That you will bless her in this time of sorrow. Why do you do these things? Why do you take them from us? We cannot know and it is not ours to know, we instead must just be there in your care. Thank you, father, and father we say—'

'Amen,' said Georgie. 'We say amen and thank you very much. In the name of the Father, Son, and the Holy Ghost.'

Hope looked up and saw Angusina, her face an expression of horror.

'That's not fair,' said Daniel. 'Angusina means well. She's not Catholic.'

'Catholic, Protestant, Hindu, Muslim whatever, it's all the same. Isn't it? What good did it ever do me? Blew the hell out of my wee country, religion,' said Georgie.

'You're from Northern Ireland then?' said Hope.

'Well, you never came up the Lagan in a bubble, did you?' Hope had no idea what that reference meant.

'You shouldn't talk so of the Lord,' said Angusina.

'I'll talk how I want, and by the way, I don't see Him coming down to give me a complaint. It's only out of you I get earache.'

'Enough,' said Daniel. 'Enough. Hope hasn't come here to listen to you two fighting it out. It's not been a good time, Hope. We've lost three of our friends and we all came here with such hopes.'

'Aye and a packet of money; you wonder where everybody is gone. Don't you? It's not like they got a refund after they died.'

'That's really quite coarse, Georgie,' said Dennis, 'even for me, and I don't mind a bit of language. Enough. You could have put something better on other than that drab jumper.'

'Oh, the fashion police are off again. Here we go. You were just the same with Joel; you never let that poor man go.'

'Well, people don't walk around in plus fours all the time. They're old-fashioned, old hat. We might be the older generation, but we can have a better style about us.'

'Style, my arse,' said Georgie. Hope saw Angusina's face give a shocked look, and then a touch of red as the anger appeared.

'I don't want to cause any problems,' said Hope.

A cup of coffee was placed into her hands. 'You're not doing anything wrong,' said Sheila. 'It's good to have you here. Mary would have enjoyed it, I'm sure. She spoke a lot of you, about you. It must have been horrible finding the arm. Is anyone with you?'

'My boss is in speaking to your manager.'

'Your boss?' said Georgie. 'What the hell is your boss doing here?'

'I suspect he came down with her. Some people are good like that, Georgie,' said Sheila.

'No, he's come down since I found the arm. You probably best know that we believe that it was taken off Mary.'

'Taken off Mary?' said Dennis. 'Like by the sea, or like a large fish?'

'What sort of fish is going to do that? And if a fish took the arm off it would eat it; it's not going to eat the body side, is it?' said Georgie.

'In the name of all that is good and holy,' said Angusina, 'can we have a little bit less of that?'

'The thing is,' said Hope, 'it looks like it was cut off with an implement, a knife, a saw, something like that.'

Suddenly, there was a silence around the room.

'Are you saying somebody killed her?' asked Georgie.

'I'm saying nothing,' said Hope. 'I'm saying there's a suspicious circumstance here that my boss is up to investigate. That's all I'm saying.'

'Joel and Natalie,' said Daniel, 'they went in a similar way. They went into the sea, too. Are you thinking that something

43

might have happened to them?'

'I am thinking nothing,' said Hope, standing up. 'Thank you all for concern around me, but look, we're at the early stages of looking into this. We don't decide what has happened until we have all the evidence, but my boss is going to want to talk to you all.'

'Well, it did seem a bit strange losing the three of them.'

'Hush,' said Daniel. 'We don't need that. We don't need wild speculation.'

'There's nothing wild about it, and you know that!' Hope saw Daniel give an enraged look towards Georgie, and Sheila made her way over to the small woman.

'That's enough, Georgie. Really enough.'

'Dead? Killed?' said Angusina. 'You're asking if they were all killed, not just simply taken from us?'

'Looks like it may not have been his providence after all,' said Georgie. Hope looked at Angusina and wondered how her body wasn't exploding from the rage that was racing around inside.

'It's all God's will,' she said firmly, as if reciting it for a mantra.

'There you go, Hope. There's the one you need to go and investigate. God did it.' With that, Daniel grabbed Georgie by the arm and whisked her out of the room.

Chapter 6

Macleod looked out of the small window and then back at the single bed. His accommodation on Eigg was far from salubrious, but it was clean and more than adequate. The woman who had showed him around had been extremely pleasant. She had cooked him a meal that night, fish with potatoes, some broccoli, and he'd wolfed it down before making a phone call home to Jane, his partner. She'd been out and about in town and talked to him for fifteen minutes about what she'd done. As he came to the end of the phone call, Macleod had no idea what she'd said.

'You're on a case, Seoras. Just go and get it done. Check in with me, tell me you're all right, but I'm not going to talk to you properly until you get this resolved because you're not here, are you?'

'I'm on Eigg,' said Seoras, and that was when he'd realised that she was completely correct. She hadn't meant anything like that. She wasn't worried about his location, but his mind was off and running. The day had been interesting, to say the least. Hope had recounted her initial meeting with the residents before showing Macleod around the building. He had then sat down to take statements from everyone and found the same detail coming up time and time again. Joel, Natalie, and Mary had all gone out to the path by the singing sands. They had signed themselves out with the book and they were doing something that many of the residents had done.

When the weather was up, the sea was breath-taking down there. Everyone said it. Everyone said they were keen to go and watch. It was like a rehearsed speech, Macleod had thought, and time and time again, he got a vivid description of the white at the top of the waves and tales of how the singing sands called to you, when you walked over them. It was almost like a brochure. Macleod wondered, did they all have this same love of the sea? Did they all get together and talk about it, and that was why he was getting this incredibly consistent description of what happened?

There had been searches each time; the lifeboat had been out around the island. They'd even brought coastguard personnel on to the island to cover the shore around it, but nothing had been found. Hope had been the first one to detect any of the three missing people. Then there was the knife or the blade that had cut Mary's arm off. Had somebody dissected the entire body? Had they cut her up and tossed her into the sea? How had she got there?

Macleod had made a phone call to Clarissa during that afternoon, figuring out the details of those staying, asking Clarissa and Ross to start delving into the backgrounds of the residents. Everyone seemed to have had a life; they all talked of being away. There also seemed to be a bit of friction within the group, and it seemed to Macleod it was deeper than a group of people who had simply been with each other less than a year should have. Maybe it was that time of life, but

46

he didn't believe that. He was getting on and he knew the difference between an ingrained prejudice and something that was just bothering you from someone you'd met recently. Only Janey Smart had seemed normal and was very cooperative in everything he'd asked.

As he stood at the window, he heard the rain beat down upon it and then made his way downstairs, where he was going to meet Hope. The landlady of the house had very generously given him a room at the back where he could set up his laptop and meet with Hope to speak privately. He had scheduled a call this evening to gather the team and was awaiting Jona's arrival at the B&B.

'Inspector? Inspector?'

'Ah, Mrs. Adams. You don't have to call me Inspector. Just Seoras will do. I'm just your guest here. I'm not investigating you.'

'Yes, well, if you're going to be like that, it's not Mrs. Adams, it's Olivia, and I've got a guest for you. Little foreign woman, quite small. Her name's Jona.'

'That's my forensic officer, Jona Nakamura. She's Asian, from Japan. Well, at least her family was, back in the day at some point,' and Macleod tried to remember exactly when she'd become part of this country but failed. Maybe his mind was starting to go.

'I've put her into the back room. Is that okay?'

'Perfect, Olivia. Perfect. Thank you. I'm just coming down now.' The woman left the room and Macleod tightened up his tie and made his way down to the back room of the house. As he entered, Olivia, the bustling landlady, was handing Jona a cup of coffee before turning back to Macleod. 'And you'll take one yourself, will you?'

'We could be here a while. Would it be possible to get a flask of something?'

'You leave it with me, Seoras.' The woman left the room.

'Does she have a husband?' asked Jona.

'What am I?' said Macleod. 'A detective?'

'Well, it doesn't take a detective to notice she's sweet on you.'

Macleod crumpled his face. He hadn't even thought about it. Now that he did, he hadn't seen a man about the place and yes, she had been very attentive to him. Still, he thought, nothing wrong with that. He would just drop in a line about phoning Jane at some point. That would set the boundaries. Boundaries, he thought. The woman hasn't even done anything. It's Jona's fault. He gazed over at the Asian woman sitting behind the table, who had her cup up to her face drinking, and who almost choked on it when she saw Macleod's face.

'She's not even—she hasn't—has she?'

'You're too easy, Seoras, too easy,' said Jona, laughing.

The door opened and Hope walked in. 'What's all this hilarity?'

Macleod looked over at Jona and gave a shake of the head. 'Don't! Let's get started. Laptops up, Hope. Can you connect the thing through? You know I have fun with it.'

'Of course, Seoras. I'll do it now while you're sitting so I can get the camera on you.' Macleod plonked himself down in a seat, only for the door to open and a large flask of coffee to be placed on the table. A cup was then placed in front of Macleod and Olivia crouched down beside him.

'This cup should be all right, it tends to keep things a lot warmer than the other ones. I'm afraid your forensic lady is going to have to make do with this one.' A thin china cup was placed in front of Jona, and then Olivia looked over at Hope.

'I'll see if I can get you a cup as well.' She disappeared from the room.

'And that's the thermal cup for the Inspector. The rest of us don't get those.'

Macleod shot a look over at Jona and she burst out laughing again. A few minutes later, Macleod was sitting in front of his laptop, watching the faces of Clarissa Urquhart and DC Ross sitting in the office at Inverness. Slowly, he recounted the day to them and watched their faces mould into disbelief as he explained how everyone's description of the place and of the sands seemed to be so very similar.

'You've got to think something's up, haven't you?' said Clarissa. 'It doesn't sound right, Seoras.'

'Indeed, it doesn't. Have we got anywhere with what I asked you to do today?'

'Not yet, Seoras. We're still looking into it. Als here, is still bringing it all together.'

Als was Clarissa Urquhart's name for DC Ross. The man was always called Ross by all his colleagues, except for Clarissa. Having joined from a different squad recently, she seemed to like to put her own mark on the group and was somewhat of a livewire.

'I need to know where the money's coming from. The manager, Janey Smart, she said her father had set this up and it was basically the income supporting her. I want to know about her father's money. I want you to check through it and make sure it's kosher. At the moment, we haven't got anything except the severed arm. That indicates foul play, but I need to know why. So, enter the backgrounds of everybody. Please do it as far you can, follow the money, follow their accounts, and see if you can get a history, passports, which country have they been in? Things like that. I need the works on this, Ross.'

'Understood, boss.'

'And what about me?' asked Clarissa. 'You know Als is better at that sort of thing.'

'You get on the phone,' said Macleod. 'That Daniel Edwards, I need to know where his money's come from. He's into the cricket world. He mentioned to me something about the MCC and connections with that. You know how to talk to the posh people; you do that. Dennis and Sheila from Glasgow, clothing gurus, get in about their business. Find out about it from those around. We don't know a lot about Georgie. Georgie Parks. And then there's Angusina, an Aberdeen tweed entrepreneur; that's where she made her money, according to her. So again, Clarissa, step into that. I'd be careful though. She says she's a woman of God. Apparently, Hope said she tried to pray with them all consistently, which is quite overt, even for someone from up my neck of the woods. So, tread lightly there, Clarissa, because you can be a bit heavy-handed to those with a fear of God.'

'Some people would say I put the fear of God into them.'

Macleod stared at the screen and then across at Hope who he could see sniggering. Jona, for some reason, had her hand across her mouth.

'Indeed,' said Macleod, 'but let's not get into that. Jona's going to be heading back up to you.'

'Yes,' said Jona. 'I need to get into a lab. There's nothing here other than the arm. I can't see the point of bringing down a forensic team at the moment when there's nothing to look at and study. If it's been a week, then there'd be nothing left. Probably has been walked over and there's really no point in the team being here. However, if you do need us, we'll be straight out, but I need some sort of crime scene before I can do anything. With regards to the arm itself, it's been cut through and I would say with force. It's a clean blow. Apologies, Hope, but it's like a big cleaver going through. The arm looks like a piece of meat would do from your butcher. You don't see any ends. It's something sharp and it's something fast.'

Macleod thought he saw Hope shiver when Jona described it and he was aware that they were talking about her aunt.

'Are you okay, Hope?' he asked.

'No, but let's get this done.' It was remarkably short and curt from her. Macleod felt for his sergeant.

'In case anybody's wondering, DS McGrath is on this investigation with me. She has assured me that she will operate professionally and maintain a distance. However, between us all, this is going to be a hard one, but we cannot let our emotions become the thing that drives this. We do it by the book. We do it the way we always do it. Is that understood?'

'Of course,' said Hope. Everyone else remained silent.

'I wasn't talking to Hope,' said Macleod. 'If Hope can maintain a detached manner the whole way through this investigation, I'll be stunned. That's why I'm here, to cover that off, to make sure that I can keep her emotional attachment out of the case. The rest of you will want to help her, but we will have to be true to being the detectives that we are. Am I understood?'

'I think I speak for us all,' said Clarissa, 'to say we want to get the bastard that did this, but we know our roles. We know our jobs. You don't have to worry.'

Macleod nodded. 'Thank you. Thank you all. Over the next few days, we're going to pull on a few strings to try and unearth what's going on this end. We'll find out who else is attached to the township. There's going to be people on the island. Are there any issues with the islanders about what is, let's face it, possibly a monstrosity to some people? They've just dumped a large retirement home for people not from the island with a graveyard and everything else besides the singing sands. Apparently, the beach is what the tourists like. I also want to know how that deal was done, because I thought most of the things here on Eigg were done by committee. But I need to get into that. All that being said, let's work fast and accurate. I'll speak to you all tomorrow. Good night, everyone.'

A curt goodnight came from Clarissa Urquhart before the screen was shut down and Macleod watched Jona slapping down the lid of her laptop.

'I won't see you in the morning,' said Jona. 'I'm going to get a good sleep, then catch the ferry. I'll be up the road but I'm on the phone whenever you need me, of course.'

'Thanks for coming down,' said Hope.

'If you need me,' said Jona. 'I don't mean about the case, I mean, if you need me, I'm on the phone.' She walked over to Hope, flung her arms around the woman, struggling to reach her and causing Hope to bend down. The height difference between the two of them was often a cause of hilarity but in this solemn moment, Macleod could see Hope taking the comfort of a friend.

When Jona stepped away, she gathered her goods and left the house, leaving Macleod and Hope in the room alone.

'What are you going to do now?' asked Macleod.

'I was going to go for a walk, go and see that path, but it's becoming wild out there.'

'Probably best if you get some sleep,' said Macleod. 'Maybe take a whisky or something.'

'I'd ask you to join me, Seoras, but I know you don't. I think it's beginning to sink in more having been down here, seeing where she was.'

'Are you okay? I mean, she was murdered by the looks of it.'

'No, I'm not okay, but you'll find who did this.'

'Well, I'm going to stay here for a bit longer, do a bit of work in this room, see what else I can tie up.'

'No, you're not,' said Hope. 'You're going to sit here and dwell on the fact that all the stories are exactly the same. You're going to try and work out who's lying to you and why.'

'Yes,' said Macleod. 'That's exactly it.'

'I'd stay up with you but I don't think I'd be much use to you in the morning.' Hope walked over, stood behind Macleod in his chair, and looked at the laptop screen in front of her. There was nothing there except the Windows background image and a couple of icons but no windows were open.

'If you close the lid of the laptop, you'll find that you don't use any power because let's face it, you're not using that thing at the moment, are you? You're using this.' With that, Hope tapped Macleod's head.

'You know me quite well, don't you?'

'That I do, Seoras, very well. And I know, unlike Jona, you won't rush over and give me a hug and hold me, telling me it's all okay.' With that, she leaned forward and wrapped her arms around his neck and gave Macleod a kiss on the cheek. 'But you're there for me, so thank you. And please keep an eye, because I'm not all right.' With that, she let go and started making her way towards the door. 'Don't stay up too late,' she said, 'not unless somebody's coming to fill up your highly thermal mug.'

Macleod shot a look at her and saw the cheeky smile.

'Good night, Hope,' he said and stared back at the Windows screen in front of him.

Chapter 7

Hope had breakfasted that morning with Macleod at the small B&B in the middle of the island. She had slept fitfully, unsure quite why, except for the obvious disturbance in her thoughts caused by her aunt's suspected murder. Macleod suggested walking up to the township, but Hope disagreed, and together they'd taken his car, parked and then run inside to the warm building, away from the rain that had started. Macleod was meeting Janey Smart again, in an effort to go through more of the detail of the building and of the residents. He was also going to look at work schedules, who on the island was involved with the township and what they did.

Hope was feeling rather downcast and asked if she could be excused from this meeting. Macleod nodded and she returned to the car, taking a large coat and putting it on. Her boots had dried out from a few days before, but they creaked as she walked along and took the path out from the rear of the township building to the hill above the singing sands.

She'd been there briefly, for it was where her aunt's coffin was buried, and right now it seemed like the place to go to.

Maybe she needed to talk to her aunt, or maybe she just needed to be near something of her. Either way, right now she couldn't face going inside the building and being bombarded by the other residents.

The coat wrapped around her, Hope trudged up the gravel path until she reached the little graveyard. The wind was picking up and the gate was swinging wildly as she reached the cemetery. Stepping inside, she closed it behind her, but turning around and looking towards her aunt's grave, she saw somebody kneeling in front of it. He too had a large coat on, Wellingtons on his feet. As he stood up, she recognised the lithe form of Daniel Edwards, the Englishman who seemed to have quite an affinity for her aunt.

'Oh, I'm sorry. I didn't think anybody else would be up here. I'll not intrude.'

'You're as entitled as I am to be up here. I got the feeling the other day you and my aunt were quite close.'

'We were,' said Daniel, 'very close. When you get to my age in life, you're not always as physically close, not in I guess the way you would with someone, but we still want to be held. We still want those quiet moments alone. We still want someone to talk to. A lot of people think we're dead when we come out here—we're just killing time before it kills us, but that's not true. Do you know what it's like to stand and feel the wind in your hair, to hear the waves crash around you? This is nature right here. It makes me feel alive. Your aunt felt the same.'

Hope watched Daniel looking at her, staring up and down, but for a moment turned away, her red hair whipping around her face. Normally when she went to work, she would tie it up in a ponytail behind her but today she hadn't. She wasn't feeling herself, not the Hope who would race out and take

56

on a case. She was more retrospective. Maybe that's why the hair hadn't been tied up, or maybe she was just wanting to feel more like Hope than Sergeant McGrath.

'You're hurting, aren't you,' said Daniel. 'I can tell, you have that same pained expression your aunt did when she was struggling with something.'

'I can't imagine she struggled with a lot out here,' said Hope. It appeared that the detective side had not gone far.

Daniel laughed shortly. 'You are what she said you are. A detective looking for what's going wrong. The way you phrase that question, you know, it's disarming. Sounds reasonable. Sounds like something somebody would say, but you're fishing for more. She was like you back in the day. Did you know that?' said Daniel.

Hope had seen pictures of her aunt. They'd all said that maybe she had been her mum because the likeness was so close. Her own mum looked very different, but Auntie Mary, the wild, bad egg of the family, although with a likeness to Hope, was always described as someone to be kept away from.

'You knew my aunt then, before here?'

'Oh, only briefly,' said Daniel. 'In passing. It's one of the things, when we came here, it was nice to have seen someone again, someone I knew.'

'Were you close before?'

Daniel turned and looked at the grave. 'No,' he said. 'We weren't. I did admire her at the time I saw her, same as I admire you, but I wasn't looking to engage the other side of her. The side that doesn't just confirm the attraction. The one that brings you close.'

Hope wondered quite what the man was on about. 'How do you mean?'

'Oh, women like you, we can look at you and think, oh yes, I want to be with that woman. I want to go with her here, there, wherever, but it's only when you get to know a woman that you decide if you really want to be with them. You know what I'm trying to say. You're not just a figure. Are you?'

Hope laughed. 'No, it's nice to hear.'

'Your aunt wasn't a figure either. She was life. She was abundant. I went swimming with her a few times down here that the others don't know about. In the summer, of course, it was a little bit better than it is today. We took a wander down to the beach and she would go across the sands, listening to me walking on them and I would listen to her, hearing the call. It was a particularly sunny day. Mary, being Mary, turned around and said, 'Let's go in.' Well, I had no wetsuit with me and I told her this. She said to me, 'Neither have I.'

'Quite something at the age of eighty to run starkers into the water. Part of me wants to tell you the tale of how then we embraced and made love on the beach, but we actually legged it back out after a minute and a half because it was freezing.' Daniel began to laugh. 'But we did cuddle that night, watching the detective program on TV. Did you know that she was so proud of you? She said, "That could be my Hope on TV, but the TV stories are not the same, are they?" That's how she thought of you. The glamorous detective.'

Hope laughed again and walked over closer to the grave. 'Why do we come here?' Hope asked. 'She's not in there. Literally not in there. I've gone to other graves and I've seen people and they talk to the person there, but the person's not there. I mean, you might as well talk anywhere.'

'You might as well,' said Daniel, 'but it's a place, isn't it? You've suddenly got nowhere to go to them. When people are alive, you can go to them. Now there's nowhere to go. Where do you go?'

'My boss would say you go to God,' said Hope.

'Well, don't ask Georgie about that one,' said Daniel.

'What's the big deal with Georgie and Angusina?'

Daniel shrugged his shoulders. 'I guess they're just from very different places.'

'I got the feeling there was something stronger. My boss did too.'

'I don't think they knew each other,' said Daniel, 'till they came here, or had even seen each other. Angusina has just got that Presbyterian mentality whereas Georgie, she's just been hacked off by the Catholic church for so long. She's beyond it. Certainly, Angusina would say she's beyond.'

'Do you believe in an afterlife?' asked Hope.

'I don't know,' said Daniel almost morbidly, but Hope thought something was bothering him.

'I mean, do you believe in a heaven? Some sort of Nirvana we go to? I know my boss does. What about you, Daniel? Is that where my aunt is?' Hope saw a flash of panic fly across the man's face before he gathered himself.

'We don't know. Sometimes I take comfort in the fact we don't know.'

Well, that was unusual, thought Hope. Daniel made his way to the edge of the graveyard, telling Hope he would leave her in peace, but as he reached the gate, she shouted over to him, 'I could actually do with a little bit of company. If you wouldn't mind, maybe we could take a walk down to the singing sands path. I could see what she found so great about this place.'

Daniel extended a hand and Hope walked across and took it and together they walked arm in arm down the gravel path and over towards where the beach lay before them. As they walked along, Daniel eventually stopped and turned to put both hands on the railing looking out. 'It was here she went,' he said.

'I know,' said Hope. 'This is where I was when I saw her. Well, I saw her shawl and that.'

'Can you feel it?' said Daniel. 'That wind, smell it. Smell the wind coming in. The spray, it's cleansing, isn't it? It's like it's making you new, taking away everything that is wrong, like the earth has picked you up again. Almost like you want to dive into that sea and let it enfold you.'

Hope looked around her. It was cold. Yes, it was breath-taking, the view, but she wasn't feeling as if life itself was being made complete by standing here. She'd always thought of herself as being very like her aunt Mary, but here was obviously something very different.

'Did you come out here often together?'

'Never the path,' said Daniel. 'I watched her standing here, but it was like I never could. I couldn't interrupt that moment of hers. She never came out with me either. The sands we went to. Oh, certainly we went to the sands. Have you been on them, heard them speak to you? It's like a call, isn't it? A call from nature. Nature saying, 'Here, come to me. Let me enfold you.' The place is breath-taking.'

'Is that what attracted you to it? Don't get me wrong. This is the isle of Eigg. It's not exactly beside any big cities or anything.'

'You can keep them. You can keep all them and all the problems. Here, we're away from all that. Here, it's just peaceful. The problems don't come for you.'

'That's what attracted you here.'

'Yes,' said Daniel. 'The brochure they put out to us when they first contacted to offer us the place, made it sound too good to be true.'

'So, you weren't looking for somewhere to retire?'

'No, but when we did, this is where we picked.'

'You said we?'

'Oh, yes. I always feel we picked it together.'

'You and my aunt?'

'No, all of us. We're a tight group. You may see Angusina and Georgie fight and that, but we're a tight group.'

'Seems awfully strange for people at the end of their life.'

'You'd be surprised the things you've got in common, surprised what you feel like you've been through. I mean, we've all had life. You're still young. You haven't had all the trials and tribulations. When we talk to each other, we know each other's problems. We're able to share, able to reminisce, able to embrace the new that's out here.'

Hope was a little bemused. It didn't seem to add up. Was this a bunch of people who wanted to march into the next life, rather than just fade away in some home, but if they were so active, why didn't they just keep going on with life? Why didn't they go somewhere else? None of them seemed to have any particular needs. She had seen the pull chains and cords that you could get assistance with. There were all these other people around to come and help, but nobody here seemed to need that much help.

'How was her hip in those last days? Did it affect her?'

'Ah, it's just one of those things,' said Daniel. 'She never let it stop her. She wasn't like that.'

The rain started to beat down and Hope felt her hair becoming wet. Daniel didn't seem bothered. Instead, he turned his face into it, letting the water soak him as a sudden deluge erupted. While they stood there over the next two minutes, Hope felt herself become utterly drenched. Then when the rain stopped, she felt the cold of the wind against her.

'Refreshing, isn't it?' said Daniel. 'That's when you know you're alive. That's when you know what's here. That's why we come out and stand here. Look at that view. On the days it's not windy, you can hear the life around here. Nature, the sea rolling in, and on the days when the wind is truly bad, you hear the crash of it as it beats down on rocks. You talked about whether I believed in heaven. This is heaven. After a life travelled, this is what heaven looks like.' Hope looked out at the sea and the sand and the rocks around her, then stared at the tall English gent. She felt she had no idea what he was talking about.

Chapter 8

After having watched Hope disappear back out to the car, Macleod pressed the bell and was approached by Janey Smart. She took him through to her office, pouring him coffee once more and sat down beside her comfortable desk ready to receive more questions from him. Macleod was in an amiable mood considering he was in the middle of an investigation, and keen to learn.

'Miss Smart, how does everybody get to be here? When did they come and visit? Did they pick up a brochure or did they pop in?'

'Oh, no Inspector, you've got to understand. It was very different. We built the place and then we looked to fill it, but we didn't want to fill it with just anyone. This needed to be a place where people got along; it needed to be a place that people spoke of as being something. This is my money, this is what makes me. If it's unsuccessful and it's not filled, I don't have any money. My father was quite strict about this; he said this is what he was going to do. In fairness, I know I enjoy it, but we had to go and find candidates.'

'How did you do that?' asked Macleod.

'Well, they needed to have certain financial clout—it's not cheap to stay here. We do provide so much but it comes with a price. We then had to look at the mix of people we would want and we asked the question, "Did we want some people who were going to sit here and look like they were in a retirement home, or is this going to be a place where you can live even though you get catered for like a retirement community would be?" You need to be an adventuring soul. We investigated the backgrounds of people. We asked who had gone away? Who travelled a lot? We came up with a rather extensive list as you can imagine.

'Then we said, "Right, everybody's got to be over eighty." That starts to narrow it down more. A lot of people in their seventies, less in their eighties who've travelled about a lot. We employed one of our counsellors to help us with that. We have a counsellor for our residence and we knew she was here on the island because she'd engaged during the building of it. We asked her and we asked our gardener to come and vet the people involved, the Islanders of Eigg for who they would want. From that process, after they'd gone through and looked at the various people, we were able to send out offers. We narrowed it down to about twenty people.

'Those twenty were sent invitations, sixteen of them responded positively. We went from there, narrowing it down until we got our little crowd of eight. I'm going to have to very soon start to offer spaces again. I haven't been pushy because our little community has to develop, but I'm going to have to go to them soon and ask who else they want in. That's one of the key things about this township—it is a township. Everybody gets a vote, everybody gets to say what's going on. This has to be somewhere people want to come to. Can you understand that, Inspector?'

'I get your business model,' said Macleod, 'but it's quite something to start involving everyone else, especially the community.'

'If the community don't like what we're doing here, then there's going to be antagonism and things aren't going to go right. My employees are all taken from the community. Therefore, they're going to pass on that disgruntlement. We try as best we can.'

'Who've you got working here?'

'Well, we have the chef, but in truth, he's fairly recent. We had to bring him in because we didn't have anyone capable of the quality of food we were looking for. It is a very high level he cooks at, and he's not cooking for many people. It's not everyone's cup of tea. We have Angus the gardener, Sarah who does the hairdressing, Moira the counsellor. Also, the other thing about Moira is she's a nurse, she can treat very basic symptoms and deal with minor issues. We have a doctor on call on the mainland who can come in if we need him. Alan organizes our supplies in town.

'I've also got Cherry who does head and muscle massage treatments. I have to tell you, Inspector, she was a bit of a find. You tend to see that thing in the bigger cities but you don't expect to find someone doing that on an island.'

'Was there a vetting process? Did you have options?'

'With the gardener position, we interviewed a couple of people, the hairdressing too, but we're not that big here on the Isle of Eigg. Therefore, a lot of people from here did get their job. To be honest, we were selling the township as employment for the island. When we first came to do this, not everybody was happy; it was very, very complicated. For a time, it looked like we weren't going to get anywhere—you can't just come and build. You obviously have to purchase the land, and, in this particular island, the islanders had to be happy.

'In fact, if I'm honest, Inspector, at the original meetings, it was quite raucous. There was total and utter defiance. They weren't going to have us here. It wasn't their idea of what an island should be. I tried to point out that why shouldn't they have a retirement home like everywhere else? Just because they're remote, why couldn't they? They didn't really seem to go with that.'

'In their defence,' said Macleod, 'it does seem that you've plonked a very expensive and albeit very elaborate and posh retirement home on them. It's not like you're picking people up from the community for a retirement home.'

'They wouldn't have enough people in the community for a retirement home,' said Janey. 'We're also providing work. I mean what do you do here? Do you turn around and say, "This is my island; I don't want anybody else near it?" If you do, it will die. What do your kids do? What do they do after school? Where do they go? They go off-island, that's what happens. You need something here and we are something that provides employment.' The woman was standing up now, marching from behind the desk, and Macleod felt he had somehow offended her or brought up past difficulties.

'I'm not here to debate the rights and wrongs of it,' said Macleod. 'I'm just looking at where the antagonism could come from. I've got one person who's had a severed arm and is missing. I've got two other people that are missing. I can't ignore any antagonism or any possible suspects.'

'I get it, Inspector, but at the time, some people on this island said things that I was not appreciative of, said things about my father and about me.'

'What things?' asked Macleod.

'Money grabbers, where did our money come from? Stuff like that. The little tart who runs the place. I gave them nothing to deserve that. I can't help the way I look.'

Macleod wondered in his own mind why they would call her a little tart? She seemed a perfectly normal woman. Yes, she was attractive, but then most women manage that before the age of thirty, unlike some men, he thought, especially himself; that's the age when you just flourish—when you look the part.

'You said it got raucous. Did it ever get violent?'

'No,' said Janey. 'It never did,' she pushed herself up on the corner of her desk. 'That was the thing that got me and my father as well. There was all this opposition. Then we said what we were paying to have the place. We paid up and over the odds. You could stick this on the coast, the west coast, for a quarter of what we paid, but we wanted here. We wanted the position beside the singing sands and we got them all talking about nature this, nature that. As soon as the money was put down, a lot of people shut up. That's what I don't get. I don't trust people's motives, especially when they're tainted by money.'

'Well, you're not getting to a lot of disagreement with me there,' said Macleod. 'The job I'm in is all about motives and money certainly does taint them. You said you sent out the invitations. How did it work from there, because you said you vetted them back down? And what were they paying?'

'The way I look at it, people have a certain lifetime to live. Now, one person you get in may last a week, the next person you get in may live another thirty years. They're all in their eighties, so be honest, if they make twenty years, they're doing well. Not many of us get to a hundred these days, do we?'

Macleod thought this was a very strange comment coming from someone in her mid-twenties. Macleod also felt that he was not in a job which he could comment about that, considering most of his clients were already dead.

'We put out these brochures and we see who came back. Now, there were some candidates who clearly didn't have the money and some that did.'

'Would it be possible to get the documentation you used?'

'I'm sure I could. We could dig it up. If you give me an hour or so, you can see why we made our decisions.'

'When you got down to your final eight, how did you pick them? Was there any number of people or were you really struggling to fill the building?'

'Oh, no. We had fourteen who came back and we actually did it by involving our local people again, but those eight people seemed especially keen according to our local sources and they got in here. In fact, we weren't quite ready for them all; when they moved, they all came quickly.'

'How did they find each other when they arrived,' asked Macleod?

'I'm amazed how well they've got on, to be honest,' said Janey. 'People would come in and you would think, "Oh, we don't know each other. Therefore, we will be polite, hellos, et cetera." No, these people get on like a house on fire, really able to talk to each other on a level that they don't do with me. I get that,' said Janey. 'I'm twenty-five; look at me. I don't fit in with them. They're polite enough, but I'm also not a resident. I am here to help and assist. I am not here to enjoy life with them and that's fine because that's my job, but they get on well together.'

'Did you get any complaints from them at any point?' asked

Macleod.

'Almost none. In fairness, when they've come in, we've had our counsellor with them as well sounding out their ideas. Our gardener has gone in and spoke to them. I've tried to introduce them to the staff, to not be staff like a care home, but staff, more like you would have in a country house, your butler, your maid, et cetera, but on a less formal level.'

'Does the weather ever bother them,' asked Macleod. 'I come from the Isle of Lewis and the winters up there are rough. I imagine it might not be quite as bad here in the Inner Hebrides, but I'm sure these small islands take a battering at times.'

'It's the west coast of Scotland,' said Janey. 'You either love it or you don't. You take the weather as it comes because of the stunning views. I've never heard any of them complain about it. In fact, they all seem to love it. They're all off out there, stepping on the singing sands, hearing the voices. Have you ever talked to any of them, Inspector?'

'Just as an interview, not recreationally,' said Macleod.

'If you do, this is what they talk about. This place, the sands, how the sands talk to them, how life is invigorated for them again. This is the place they want to be. I have to say we picked the right eight people. It's just a pity we've lost three of them.'

'Do you actually believe that they simply got caught up and went over the side in the weather?' asked Macleod. Janey jumped off the desk, stared at him.

'Absolutely. I don't know how Mary's arm has been cut off. Maybe it went across a certain object or something. Why would anyone come out here and kill anybody here and to do it in such a way? Along that path? You're suggesting to me that people are going out and lobbing them off? It's crazy. They're all so happy here. My workers are happy because it's

69

employment. It's money coming in. We pay well. I am at a loss with what you're trying to suggest to me, Inspector. I know you have a job to do, and I know you come in with a suspicious mind and I do not blame you for that, but I don't see it at all.'

'Forgive me for what I'm about to say, but how quickly do you have to replace a resident? You talk about the idea of some of them living twenty years.'

'I budget for them to live a minimum of ten years. Okay? I cost it out for ten years. I will be paying everything and looking after these people. Therefore, the price they paid at the start covers that on average. If you're asking, am I starting to bump off my residents because I cannot afford the bills, that is absolute nonsense. Now, I'm on the plus with it. Check my books; I have no financial difficulties. This is a win, Inspector, for everyone.'

Macleod nodded and thanked the woman for her time, stood up and shook her hand. He said he'd be back, but in the meantime, he was going to go and speak to the residents. Once Macleod stepped out of the office, he returned to the communal room and walked over to look out of the large windows. Yes, the view was spectacular. Yes, it had the special beach that made sounds as you walked across it, but how much money to be here? Janey Smart said she wasn't bumping people off, but she was talking as if she was covering the bills. What if you could get people to pay more? The people here were old.

But the idea that you disappeared off the side, fell down a cliff in wild weather. It certainly was a good cover if you wanted to get another resident in and earn in more money. They must have been paying in the tens of thousands for this, at least, in fact, probably more like hundreds of thousands. A couple extra of those above what you budgeted would seem

70

to set you up. Macleod could see motive, the financial motive, but he had no firm evidence. He had nothing saying what had happened here. He couldn't even prove that they hadn't fallen over off the rocks themselves. There would be a lot more digging to do.

Chapter 9

'Are you coming with me on this one?' Ross looked over his desk at a senior colleague who seemed to have a lot of paper around her.

'Yes, I'm coming,' said Clarissa. 'Just give me a moment. It's one of the things—you talk to people, you sit and you make notes, and then this note links to that note, that note links to this note. After a while, the paper just doesn't fold. We need 3D paper.'

'I think that's why the boss does it all in his head,' said Ross. 'I find a spreadsheet helps, but we need to go. The man said half ten.'

'The man can say what he wants. He'll speak to us when we're there.'

'That's a wee bit unfair. It's not like he's a suspect.'

'Okay, okay,' said Clarissa, who was tidying all her paperwork up into one pile of rumpled sheets.

'Have you got anywhere?'

'I'm still tracing people. You get through; you find out they weren't there but talked to people there. They then say, 'Oh, this person knows them better.' You're waiting on phone calls.

You're working through but it just takes time, Als.'

'Then maybe you need a break,' said Ross. 'Come on.'

Clarissa stood up and put a scarf around her neck. She then wrapped up a large shawl around her. 'Well, it is getting bitter.'

'I just thought a big coat would be more practical. If you had to run after someone.'

'What do you think you're here for?' said Clarissa. She smiled cheekily and strutted out of the office. 'Come on, Als. We'll be late.'

The pair headed downtown to the offices of a bank just off the high street. Clarissa didn't recognise the name, but as Ross said, they weren't into personal accounts. They dealt mainly with companies, people requiring significant sums of money, backing this and that, making their money off loans and interest.

'Well, they seem to have done all right,' said Clarissa, walking in through the front doors, admiring a rather snappy office with a woman and a man sitting behind a desk at the front. The young man stood up, made his way out from behind the desk, and placed his hand out, waiting for Clarissa to shake it. 'Hey, good morning. My name's John, how can I help you?'

'We have an appointment,' said Ross from behind Clarissa. 'Here to see a Mr. Kean.' He flashed his credentials.

'Ah, yes, you're the police officers. Delighted to meet you. If you'll come this way, I'll take you directly up to Mr. Kean.'

The man departed the front office with the officers in tow, made his way up a set of stairs before depositing them in a small waiting area. 'Can I get you some coffee?'

'I'd rather have some tea,' said Clarissa. 'If that's available.'

'English breakfast, lapsang souchong, jasmine, Earl Grey, Lady Grey? What would you like?'

'Lapsang souchong,' said Clarissa, and the man nodded before turning to Ross.

'Just a black coffee, thank you.'

'Americano, then. I'll be with you directly with those. I think Mr. Kean will be ready for you in just a minute.'

'Lapsang souchong,' said Ross. 'I didn't know you drunk smokey tea.'

'I don't,' said Clarissa. 'Just thought I would see what it was like.' Ross shook his head. Working with Clarissa was certainly different from his last colleague. He watched her gaze around the offices, taking in every detail. She was eccentric, but she was also very thorough.

'You know you said they had money, Als. I'm not so sure they do. Some of this decor. That's actually the cheap stuff over in the corner; you'd never tack the ends like that if you paid money for those. No, they did this on a budget.'

'I'm sure most offices are done on a budget these days.'

'Yes, it's just a bit of a come-down from the art world. Anyway, Als, this looks like us.'

The man arrived with a tray which included a cafetière, announcing that Mr. Kean was ready for them. He then led them forward, knocked a small door, and being told to come in, he pushed the door open, allowing the guests to enter first before setting the tray on a table in the corner. 'May I introduce Mr. Kean, the director of the firm?'

'That's lovely, John. Thanks very much. My name is Nicholas Kean. Delighted to meet you. I hope you've been treated well. If you'll take a seat in the corner, I'm sure I can help you with whatever business you may have with us.'

Ross noted that the man's hands were agitated as he fidgeted, but his face belied that, and he wondered if the man played poker.

'Thank you for your time,' said Clarissa. 'I'm Detective Sergeant Clarissa Urquhart. This is Detective Constable Alan Ross. Here's the paperwork, so to speak.' Clarissa pulled out her credentials in a small wallet, but the man waved it away.

'Don't be ridiculous,' he said. 'Sit down. I see you're drinking that smokey stuff. I'm glad somebody is. We bought it in and nobody seems to touch it.'

Ross caught a whiff of it and understood why.

'Always a favourite of mine,' said Clarissa and ignored the raised eyebrow from Ross. Once they were seated, Ross began to question the man about the retirement home on Eigg.

'We're here to speak about the Singing Sands Later But Better Township on the isle of Eigg. I take it you're familiar with it.'

The man shook his head, but not in denial, more in frustration. 'Really? Do you want to talk about that? Okay. It was all a bit funny, wasn't it?'

'I'm not quite sure what you mean, sir. We're coming at this completely cold. Any details you could furnish about the process and your involvement would be greatly appreciated.'

The man sat back and Ross noticed his hands were much more at ease now. Had he been wondering if they were coming to talk about something else?

'Our involvement was really as the finance behind it. I say the finance, but the builders, Smart Construction, they had the money. It's just the way it works, looking for the upfront loan. We got tied into it for a significant amount of money. We also had a hand in the process of what was going on just from a due diligence point of view. The whole idea was to build what was quite an expensive complex, and then sell off lifetime care, so to speak. We would put up a large block of money and then large blocks of money would come back in, once the residents had taken up. It was a bit of a gamble. In one sense, you had to guess how long each one would live. You would make enough, in the short term, it would look good. In the longer term, maybe not so good, so they were taking out some finance around it. We sat on board to make sure that they weren't going to get gazumped and suddenly have not enough people taking up because our money was tied up in it. Mr. Smart has a significant amount of holdings, but like with all businesses, cash flow is king and that's what we were needed for. Not many people have the money being talked about.'

'What sort of money were you talking?'

'Several million upfront,' said Mr. Kean. 'You see, the weird thing was how they were choosing the people to come in. Most retirement homes, you put out adverts, whatever and people join and you get paid. A lot of them, they have the NHS paying in for the care or it's coming from the funding that people have in their bank accounts. That's paid monthly and it's pretty solid. One disappears, next one comes in. That's how you keep going, standard overheads, et cetera. But this was slightly different, large chunks of money up front. There were also indications that they wanted the right people. It just felt a bit funny. I sat in on most of it.'

'How did you find it?' asked Clarissa.

'Convoluted, if I was going to use a professional word, convoluted. If I was going to say it in the vernacular, it was a pile of crap. They went out, started to pick people. I mean, they had people off the island picking who was going to come in. People with no experience of running businesses, sitting there saying this is the best candidate, this person was, this person wasn't. I mean, what was that about? They didn't advertise. They selected people. We're not a head hunter firm here looking to get your next process manager or your next senior accountant. This is a retirement home.'

'Did you intervene at any point?'

'No, I didn't, and that was simply because I couldn't find anything to intervene on. If I was sitting saying the money's not going to come here, I could have acted, but they got their money. They got everyone in, but it took time. That was the only thing about it. We were out of pocket a bit longer and it cost the Smart company a bit more because of that.'

'So, do they owe you money still?'

'No. Once it all worked, Mr. Smart paid everything back. I mean, we did all right out of it, made good money, and I think Smart's doing okay with it as well. As far as I could see, there was nothing irregular.'

'No, sir, there's nothing irregular we can see about it either,' said Clarissa. 'We're just here for some background information. Unfortunately, there's been a death at the care home that needs looked into. We're just pursuing basic inquiries at the moment as to how everything happened.'

'A death at the care home . . . you kind of expect that, though, don't you?'

'It depends on the type of death, sir,' said Ross, 'but I take your point. You say the process was convoluted. How exactly did they pick people? You said the islanders were involved.'

'Yes. Originally the islanders were a real sticking point in actually getting that place built, but the money involved and the jobs incoming into the island was lavish, to say the least. I think that's what swayed them. But Smart was okay on that because he was going to make enough off it. When they picked the people out, there was some sort of psychologist I think involved. There were the island people and Janey Smart was overseeing it. That's the person who was going to manage it, Smart's daughter, but I don't believe she actually made the choices.

'To be frank, I was sitting there listening to all this, and I got bored. Ended up going out to lunch with Smart himself. We didn't come back for about three hours and they still hadn't made their decisions by then. In the end, they tied it down to eight people. One of the islanders was quite significant in making those decisions. I was quite surprised because they then had to all agree on it, all the people they were looking to entice. They sent out the paperwork, they got back, yes, they wanted to be in it, picked them out and said, "Here's all the other people going. Are you happy with this?" and they got a yes. I mean, there's two sides to that, isn't there?'

'Two sides,' said Clarissa. 'How do you mean?'

'Well,' continued Mr. Kean. 'You could either sit there and say, "I don't know any of these people, so what the heck, let's just go anyway." Or you go and you have a serious look at them. If I was going to go and live somewhere like that, given it's an island, it's off the mainland, there's not a lot around you and you're going to be in a complex with these eight other groups of people, I want to know I'm going to get on with them, especially if I'm intending to die out there.'

The man was abrupt, pretty blunt, and Ross felt that was probably what was needed in most of his work. He certainly wasn't selling the romantic dream of a retirement home on a Scottish island, but it did make Ross think the process seemed a little strange. Maybe the process needed further investigation.

'So basically, everything went smoothly for you?' said

Clarissa.

'Oh, no, it wasn't smooth. I mean, it's not the worst I've been in. There was one point we nearly pulled out.'

'What was that?'

'Well, there was the point when they were taking it to the islanders and there was the whole big debate down in the village hall and the islanders weren't going to have it. That's when the extra money was put in. The islanders needed talking round. I believe somebody, one of the islanders did it. They all seemed to be quite keen once the money was put in. Although that one who swayed it, was quite keen beforehand.'

'Do you know their name?' asked Ross.

'No,' said Kean. 'I don't get bogged down in the minutiae like that. It wasn't really my place. I was just there as a watching brief, just making sure that with the amount of money we were putting out, nothing was going sidewards. It's just one of those things you have to do.'

'Well, thank you,' said Ross. 'You've been most helpful.'

'No, absolute pleasure. If you need anything else on that, by all means, just call the office. Do what I can for you.'

Kean stood up, made his way round the table they were sitting at and waited for Clarissa to rise. As she did so, wrapping her scarf around her neck again, she smiled at the man.

'Thank you very much. You've been most helpful and most kind and considerate with the tea and coffee.'

'But you haven't touched yours,' said Kean.

'No,' said Clarissa, 'I haven't. Interesting smell, though.' And with that, she walked out of the office. The man stared at Ross, who shrugged his shoulders before putting a hand out and shaking Mr. Kean's.

Once out in the street, Clarissa stopped Ross.

'Als, did you notice something?'

'I noticed a few things,' said Ross. 'But what are you talking about specifically?'

'Convoluted process. All very strange. It's not right. Is it? I wonder who the person was who drove the decision? I wonder, were they part of the group that were looking at it? Were they involved with the names as well? I think I need to go and talk to some more people. I get the feeling this one won't be solved in your spreadsheets.'

Ross was always ready to concede that spreadsheets were not everything, but he was also happier with them, so he'd be content to let Clarissa chase down the people on this one.

'Who are you thinking of?'

'I'm thinking that we may need to look into the builders, Smart Construction. I'll get after the people; you get after the company. And also the people who were there,' said Clarissa. 'If they had to pick these certain names and get them all together, we really need to know why. We need the backgrounds of these people. I think this is where we're going to solve it, Als. I think it's in the detail of the people involved.'

'You really think there's something strange at work here? I mean, it could be just something benign, something a bit odd.'

'It could be, but a severed arm? And Macleod went straight down. Something's up, Als, something.'

'Well, we'll follow it through, but Clarissa. Lapsang souchong? Seriously?'

'Was a nice smell. I'll give it that.'

Chapter 10

Macleod sat down to a meal of potatoes, chicken, and cauliflower and was happily tucking into it when he heard a knock at the front door of his bed and breakfast. His landlady answered the door and a breathless Hope appeared inside the small dining room, her hair looking dishevelled.

'You need to grab your coat, Seoras. Something's up.'

'It can't wait until I get this down me?' he asked.

'No,' said Hope. 'It can't. One of them is missing, the American woman, Nancy, she's gone.'

Macleod looked out of the window of the dining room and saw the rain beginning to hammer against it. A few trees in the area were buckling, bending over.

'We're about to hit a storm. Aren't we?' He queried.

'We're not about to hit it,' said Hope. 'It's happening.'

'How long's she been gone?'

'Two hours, but she's not in the home. Given these current circumstances, I think we need to start looking.'

'Does she ever go anywhere else?'

'Where else do you go? It's the Isle of Eigg.'

'They do have shops and things. Not many. She might have gone for a wander.'

'A wander, Seoras? Come on, look at it.' Macleod dug his fork into his chicken, cut about a third of it off, picked it up, and shovelled it into his mouth. Hope watched him chew it rapidly before grabbing his cup and taking a large drink of water.

'Okay, Hope, let's go. I'll meet you outside.' Macleod returned to his bedroom, grabbed his long coat, and put on a pair of wellington boots that he always had with him these days. Once in the car, he let Hope drive up to the retirement home, the wipers working overtime to clear the pouring rain off. Although it was teatime, Hope already had the lights on and darkness was rapidly ensuing.

'We've checked everywhere inside the retirement home?'

'Yes,' said Hope. 'I got hold of Janey Smart. She opened up every door. We went through everywhere.'

'There's nothing to find at all?'

'No.'

'What about her husband?' asked Macleod.

'He's a gibbering wreck. Some of the others said she disappeared out.'

'Did she sign out?'

'I didn't even think of looking, Seoras. I was so wrapped up in getting everywhere searched and getting you.'

'Don't worry. It's okay. You're under a heck of a lot of pressure now. Go and start organizing a search party around the island. Take care. Phone the coastguard and see if the lifeboat will come down and do a coastal search. Or a helicopter, whatever we can get out in this weather.'

'Okay. Will do. What are you going to do?'

'I'm going to talk to her gibbering wreck of her husband, some of the other residents, see if anybody saw where she went. You'll cover the ground out there much better than I will, but anything I find from them, I'll give you a call. Has anybody tried the path?'

'I took a quick look out there, couldn't see anything. I haven't been down around the rocks or that.'

'Well, that may be somewhere to go.'

The car pulled up in front of the retirement home, and Macleod jumped out, running through driving rain. As he entered the building, Janey Smart was in the common room and she ran over to the Inspector as he got there.

'Any sign yet?'

'No,' said Macleod. 'Where's her husband?'

'He's in his room. He's locked the door, stamping his feet and everything.'

'Show me to it,' said Macleod. Janey ran and Macleod struggled to keep up with her as he went along the corridors. As they got to the man's room, he could see the other residents gathering outside.

'This is it, Inspector,' said Janey, slightly out of breath. Macleod pulled up behind her, stopped momentarily, sucking in the air. When he was ready, he rapped the door.

'Mr. Griffin, this is Detective Inspector Seoras Macleod. I need to speak to you about your wife, sir. I need to talk to you.'

'Why is he like this?' asked Angusina, the Hebridean woman.

'Probably done her away himself,' said Georgie. Macleod turned to the diminutive Irish woman.

'That can stop right now. The man's probably distressed given what's happened to previous people. Now, if you're not going to be useful, get out of here.'

Georgie stared at the Inspector, but eventually retreated. Then tall Daniel Edwards took hold of Angusina and walked down the corridor with her, leading her out towards the common room.

'Mr. Griffin, I need to talk to you and urgently about your wife.' Macleod could only hear sobs from inside the room.

'Janey, have you got a key?'

'I do, but we only use them in emergencies.'

'I'm a Detective Inspector and this is an emergency. Open that door!'

Janey looked slightly put out, but she reached into her pocket and pulled out a key, opening up the door for Macleod.

'Just stay out here,' he said. He rapped the door again before opening it. Inside, he saw a large suite. On a sofa, towards the middle of the room, a man sat crying. Around him was a splendid kitchenette, a bedroom area on the far side of the room, as well as an alcove leading to what Macleod thought would be the bathroom area. He walked quietly round the sofa and stood before Jake Griffin.

'I'm aware you might be distressed, sir, but I do need to ask you some questions.'

The man looked up, crying. He said nothing but then put his head back down. Macleod knelt on the floor, looking up towards the man. 'You're going to need to talk to me. If I'm to find her, you need to talk to me. Did she say what she was doing?'

'No,' he said. 'No.'

'Was she wearing anything different,' Macleod asked.

'Her coat. She had her coat on, the big one. We said, when we came here, she'd need a big coat. The winters, they can be bad. They told me they can be rough.'

'Yes, they can be rough. What colour of coat?'

'Red. It was a red coat.'

'Anything else?'

'No, I don't remember anything else. She said she was going out. I said, do you want me to come and she said, no. It's not unusual.'

'Does she walk a lot on her own?'

'We both do. We all walk alone. Don't we? We all go out alone.'

'Did she say where she was going? Jake, where has she gone?'

'She told me she could hear the children.'

'What?' said Macleod. 'What children? There's no children here. It's a retirement home.'

'She said she could hear the children. They're in the sand. The children are in the sand. They're coming back to us. They're coming back. The children came back to her. Do you understand?'

'No, I don't,' said Macleod. 'What children?'

The man's shoulders slumped, and he began to cry again. Macleod pitied the man, but he needed information. He reached forward and lifted his chin up.

'What children?'

'The children of the sand. She's gone out to the sands. She gone out to the cliff. The call on the sand. She said she heard them yesterday. She was down on the beach, and they said to her, they spoke.'

'What did they say to her?' asked Macleod, hoping that this line might bring out something.

'They spoke. They spoke, Inspector.' With that, the man reached forward grabbing Seoras by the shoulders, almost shaking him. 'They spoke. They haven't spoken in a long time.'

Macleod was confused. It felt like he was in some sort of horror movie, but the man had seemed utterly lucid the day before. Was it the shock of his wife disappearing? In his head, was he thinking about things, worried that she may become another victim?

'What children?' asked Macleod, but the man began to sob bitterly. He was shaking, and then suddenly collapsed on the sofa.

'First aider,' shouted Macleod to the door. Janey popped her head in. 'Get a first aider, somebody medical in here now. He's not good.'

Macleod tried to lift the man back up, saw his head rolling, his eyes spinning. He was breathing, but he seemed disoriented. It was two minutes before Janey ran back in with a woman behind her.

'This is Moira. She doubles as our nurse.' The black-haired woman ran around the sofa, crouched down beside Macleod, and began looking Jake Griffin over. She sat him back in the sofa.

'Calm, Jake. Stay calm. Let's just stay calm.' The woman took the man's hand and rubbed the back of it. Then she reached up examining each eye, pulling back the lid.

'I think he's just agitated, Inspector. I'll stay with him if you need me to.'

'I think it's best. I won't ask him any more questions because he wasn't giving me much of an answer, and it seemed to agitate him. Janey, take me to the book, the one that residents sign when they leave.'

'Of course, Inspector. You need anything else, Moira?' she asked.

'I'll be fine, Janey. I think he'll be okay.'

Macleod walked swiftly behind Janey as she made her way to a book at the far side of the common room. Flicking back the pages, she opened up the current day, and Macleod scanned the names. Most of the residents had been out at some point during the day despite the poor weather, but he noticed that none had gone out together or at the same time. The last entry, however, was Nancy Griffin, and there was no return time written.

'It looks like she's gone out on the path,' said Janey. 'That's pretty normal.'

'He said that she was telling him about the voices of children. Do you know anything about children? Do they have any children?' asked Macleod, quickly.

'As far as I know, they're childless, part of the attraction of being here,' said Janey. 'Sorry, Inspector. I'm none the wiser.'

Macleod took out his mobile and placed a call through to Hope.

'I think she's gone out on the path,' said Macleod.

'I was there earlier,' said Hope, 'and we couldn't see anyone. I've got some people from the village coming. We'll be up there in about ten minutes.'

'Any luck with the coastguard?'

'I'm not sure they can get a helicopter out in this. The wind is so bad. The lifeboat may come out, but it's going to be touch and go. These high winds are a problem. We also can't confirm it's on the sea. I said to him, 'Can we get anybody over here to help search?' Again, it's unlikely anyone's going to travel. We may have to bed down for the night.'

'I'll go out now, myself,' said Macleod.

'Not on your own. If these winds are high, you need somebody with you.'

'Of course,' said Macleod. 'I'll take someone with me. We'll see you out in that path in about twenty minutes then.'

'I will. Seoras, take care.'

Macleod closed the phone call and looked at Janey Smart beside him. 'Have you got a decent coat? We need to go out and have a look at the track.'

'You want me to go in that, Inspector? Is it safe? We've lost three of our residents off that path in weather like this.'

'That's why I'm not going out on my own,' said Macleod. He sent Janey Smart running to her office for a coat. A few minutes later, they hiked along the path looking down towards the sands in the gloom of the fading day.

'Are you okay, Inspector? This is wild.'

Macleod agreed. As he walked along the path, his hand kept a firm grip on the rail. They reached a particular corner, the one that it was believed that the residents had fallen over. Macleod put a second hand on the rail, telling Janey to do the same. He gazed down into the gloom below. He could barely see the sea, the white spray being the most evident part as the water crashed against the rock.

Looking off to his left, he saw the beach, the tide running fast onto it, but he could see no one. He tried his penlight in the gloom, but the distance was too far and the beam not strong enough. Several times he felt the wind at his back, felt his body moving. A part of him believed he could get blown off the path, even over these railings.

'Can we move back?' said Janey. 'I'm really not happy about this.'

'Of course,' said Macleod. 'Keep a hand on the rail, whatever you do.'

Slowly, they made their way back, the driving rain now

soaking Macleod's trousers so much so he could feel the cold across his knees. As they walked down towards the beach, he saw a large jacket coming towards him, a number of other people behind all carrying torches.

'Seoras,' shouted Hope. 'Where have you been?'

'Checked the path. She's not up there. Can't see a thing, Hope. Let's get a quick look on the beach.'

Together, the small party made their way down to the beach and spent the next thirty minutes walking around. Macleod could barely hear the sand over the driving wind and he stumbled several times as he was almost blowen off his feet.

'Don't want a boat out in this. I don't want anything unnecessary,' said Macleod. 'If she's gone into that sea, she's gone.'

'Why on earth would you be out here on a day like this?' said Hope. 'This is crazy.' Macleod watched one of the searchers, a man from the village, as he got blown off his feet and into some rocks. Hope ran over and there was a cut across the man's face but he seemed to be okay. Macleod suspected the wind was picking up, even more.

'Back,' he said. 'We go back. Get these people home. We're going to have to bed down for the night.'

'A good idea, Seoras', said Hope. They could barely hear each other above the howling wind, but together, the small party made their way back, many holding on to each other until they got inside the retirement home. Once inside, Macleod thanked the people for their efforts but told them to go home and to stay safe. He'd call them again if they were required once the winds had died down.

'This is crazy,' said Hope. 'What on earth is she doing out there?'

'I don't know,' said Macleod, 'but I'll tell you something, Hope. I don't believe the answer is going to be out there. The answer is in here with these people and I'm not going to back down until I find out what it is.'

Chapter 11

Macleod stood at the door of the residential home looking out at the wild sea. The skies had cleared somewhat briefly, and the rain had stopped, but the wind was still blowing as wildly as before. You could see every tuft of the grass straining, being flattened by this rolling wind that whipped in off the sea. Macleod was sure that he could feel the windows shake every now and then.

Macleod decided not to return to his B&B that night, instead choosing to remain up at the home to talk to the residents. Many of them were still up, attending to Jake, but also in somewhat of a tizzy themselves. Janey Smart had not gone back to her attached apartment, and sat across the common room from Macleod. He could see she was fretting, deeply worried, and who wouldn't be, as this was the fourth resident to have disappeared within the last a couple of months.

'Would you like more coffee, Inspector?' asked Janey, standing up. Macleod didn't, but he thought it would give the woman something to do.

'Of course, just black please. Now, maybe you could check everyone. Go around the rest of the residence, see if they need anything else. Most of them are gathered in the common room as well.' Macleod heard a weeping over his shoulder and Jake was being brought in by Daniel, to sit on one of the main sofas.

'I thought it was best that we all gathered together,' said Daniel.

'The man looks positively shaken to me,' said Macleod. 'I think he'd be better served by getting some sleep.'

'He won't sleep,' said Daniel. 'How's he going to sleep when his wife's out there?' Daniel stepped closer. 'I have tried,' he whispered, 'but the man won't have it. Better him here amongst friends than back in his room.'

Out here amongst friends, thought Macleod. *But is he? There's someone here not a friend.* But he was struggling with something in his mind. Why did they all go out on their own? Why this walk to that part of the path? Why was it never a pair of them? He turned away and received a coffee in his hand from Janey Smart. He thanked her and went to sit in the corner, to ponder on his thoughts.

'Do you mind if I join you, Inspector? You're looking alone sitting there.'

Macleod looked up and saw Georgie wrapped up in a dressing gown. She didn't wait for a reply, but instead dumped herself down beside Macleod.

'Is there no way they can get anyone out? I thought these helicopters could operate in most weather.'

'The helicopter and the lifeboat have said they need the weather to improve. There's nothing I can do about that. I'm not a pilot, either of a helicopter or a boat. You have to take their word for it these times, as much as you want things. I can't endanger the lives of those who are going to save.'

'She'll not stand a chance out there. I mean, if she's come off that path, the way those waves are coming in and all that.'

'Keep your voice down,' said Macleod. 'I agree it looks grim, but her husband's over there.'

'Well, it's probably best to hear it straight then, isn't it?'

'No, it probably isn't, Georgie. Please now, tell me, what is this obsession with out there?'

'Obsession? I wouldn't say any of us had an obsession, Inspector, but it is quite something, isn't it? When you walk along the sand and you hear it singing.'

'Jake said his wife had heard the children. Do you know what that was about?'

Georgie fixed him with a stare before shaking her head. 'You hear the sound of singing, Inspector; maybe it sounded like children to her.'

'But why would she want to hear children?'

'Maybe it's just us getting old, Inspector. You see the young ones, it reminds you of your youth, that sort of thing. I remember being a wee girl running up and down the Falls Road. A long way from there now, you know.'

'When was the last time you were back there?' asked Macleod.

'Oh, I've never been back since I left as a wee girl. Oh, I must only have been about seventeen.'

'Where did you go?' asked Macleod.

'I went off to be a nun, but I wouldn't want to be one of them nuns who just kicked about the place. I went off overseas doing aid work.'

'And whereabouts?'

'Well, I worked all over Africa, quite a bit of it at the start, then I came back—gave up being a nun. Probably missed the liquor. I like to be drinking at times like these.'

Macleod nodded, never comfortable with the mention of alcohol.

'What about you, Inspector? You never like a wee drink?'

'I don't touch it. I don't trust it,' said Macleod.

'Your accent's awful similar to Angusina's. Are you from that part of the world, too?'

Macleod nodded. 'Lewis, not Harris.'

'Look, well, that explains a lot.'

'What do you mean by that?' asked Macleod.

'Well, quite frankly, your face is like a smacked ass. You never seem happy at all. I know you're investigating something, but there's no need not to break out the odd smile.'

Macleod was becoming distinctly annoyed with the woman, but he wasn't going to give her the pleasure of firing back at her. Instead, he turned around, gave a broad smile and stood up. 'If you'll excuse me, I'm just going to talk to some of your fellow residents.' He strode over to Daniel, who was taking a cup of tea by a table in the corner.

'Excuse me, Daniel, but Nancy said she was taking a walk out. She said she'd been hearing the children. That's what Jake kept saying, she'd been hearing the children.'

'Yes, it's got me, that one, Inspector. I don't get that either. I mean you go down to the sands and it's fabulous. You hear it sing, but it's not children. I don't know. Maybe she'd been struggling, gone in the mind, a touch of dementia.'

'I spoke to her the other day. I interviewed her right here and she didn't seem to be losing her mind in any capacity,' said Macleod.

'Sometimes it doesn't show, does it? And we hide it so well. No one wants to admit that they're forgetting things, that certain images are coming to them.'

'I thought that generally happened to people on their own, people that were lonely. They saw things, images of the past, that are made up of people that are not around.'

'Well, that is true,' said Daniel, 'but I don't think it was always people on their own.'

'Have you ever been anywhere with children?' asked Macleod.

'What do you mean?' Asked Daniel.

'Where they would sing?' The man shook his head, 'Or maybe they would cry out,' said Macleod. There was a momentary pause, a slight hesitation. 'Are you sure you haven't encountered something like this?'

'It's just something you bring back from back in the day. My brother was run over. I remember him screaming.'

'Was he killed?' asked Macleod.

'No, no. He was on his bike, knocked over. Hurt himself quite badly, but he was screaming and I think that's what did it. That's just set me back, just remembering that there.'

Macleod didn't believe a word of it. 'Well, I'm sure that's traumatic for you, but she said that she could hear the children. They were coming back to her. Did she ever tell a story where that would make any sense?'

'Well, we've not been here that long together and no. I'm afraid Jake used to do more of the talking than Nancy, one of the wives that's happy to sit in the background, you know?'

Macleod could see that his line of attack wasn't going to pay any dividends, but he was sure Daniel was holding something back. He walked over to where Jake was sitting on the sofa with Hope beside him. The man was a perpetual cycle of tears, then reminiscence, then complete silence. Macleod sat beside him and the man barely looked up at him.

'Tell me again,' said Macleod, 'what she said.'

'She heard the children, Inspector. The children. They were in the sand. They're coming back. They're coming back, Inspector.'

'Do you know what that means, Jake, when she said that?' The man doubled up again and began to cry. Dennis and Sheila, the clothing gurus from Glasgow, were keeping out of the way with Dennis having his eyes transfixed on the weather outside. Macleod called them over.

'Sorry to bother you,' he said. 'It's just that Jake here keeps saying that Nancy talked of children out in the sand.'

There was a flicker across Dennis's face, but Sheila waved her hand up quite dismissively. 'She was prone to a little bit of that, Inspector, saying things. She's quite the artist. If you go into her room, you'll see these drawings and pictures. She always talked about things being inside inanimate objects, bringing a life to them. Those sands, you can hear them sing and I wouldn't be surprised that she thought it was like children's voices. Maybe she was looking at a choir.'

'She said they were coming back to her. Back to her!'

'Well, maybe she'd missed it,' said Dennis. 'Sometimes you go down and you walk across and it's not the same sound. I've always wondered that, quite how that works.'

Macleod could see the same stonewall faces. There was something there. Something he needed to chisel at. He turned back to Jake. 'Who are these children, Jake? Tell me.'

'Do you think that's necessary?' said Dennis. 'You seem to be forcing the issue on a man that's clearly struggling.'

'I appreciate your concern, Dennis, but as an inspector, I'll decide what I need to ask and at the moment, I think it's very relevant.'

'To be honest,' says Dennis, 'You might be better letting him sleep and then talk to him about it afterwards. He doesn't look that great.' Macleod did note that the man was white and clearly emotionally traumatized. 'Maybe me and Sheila could get him to bed. That would probably be more sensible, then you could talk to him in the morning when he gets up. I think we're all a little tired, Inspector. Let's be honest.' Dennis leaned forward to Macleod's ear. 'We're not going to find her tonight, are we? This weather won't blow through until tomorrow. She's probably gone.'

Macleod knew the man was telling the truth, and nodded.

'Okay,' said Macleod. 'Take him back to his room. See if you can get him to sleep.' As soon as Dennis lifted Jake to his feet, Georgie appeared along with Daniel, and it was only Angusina left in the corner of the room. Macleod walked over to the woman in the plaid skirt and rather dour, brown jumper.

'Mrs. Macleod, I'm sorry to bother you, but it seems you were rather better prepared than the others. Most of them are out in their dressing gowns, but you're still up.'

'You don't come out here walking around in your dressing gown, Inspector. I thought you would've known that. We have better standards back where we come from.'

Macleod couldn't quite see how Angusina running around in her dressing gown was any source of attraction for anyone, but he could fully understand if she was brought up that way, why she would act accordingly.

'Jake keeps saying about the singing sands reminding Nancy of children. Children coming back to them. Do you know anything about that?'

Angusina turned and with fierce eyes, looked at Macleod, 'Can't you let the woman be at peace? She's obviously dead

97

out there. Nobody's coming back from that.'

'We don't really have a lot of hope there, then do we?' said Macleod. 'And not a lot of sympathy, either'

'We rely on the Lord's providence, you know that,' said Angusina. 'These Americans, they don't look to him. She was telling me that the games they play, their football and that, they have them on Sundays.'

'A lot of sports played on a Sunday night,' said Macleod.

'Not on the islands.'

'It's a different day,' said Macleod. 'Even I can see that and trust me, I was brought up to the book.'

'Do you know that not one of them has a copy here? Not one of them? I tried to tell them. I tried to tell them to get themselves in order, to look to the Lord, but they don't.'

'What about the children, Mrs. Macleod? Tell me about the children.'

'I don't know anything about the children, whoever she's worried about.' The response was less of a denial and more of a wall being built up. 'Don't ask me about that again.'

Macleod wondered if he should press this point. 'It's not the sounds though, is it?' he said.

'Inspector, people hear voices in the sands. We hear a lot of things. It's not really important, is it?'

'Oh, I think it is.' Angusina turned her head, stood up, and announced that she'd need to take care of Jake as well, leaving just Hope and Macleod standing together. 'Useful session, was it?' asked Hope.

'What do you make of these children, the voices in the sand? Every time I ask about it, it just get dismissed. Everybody's rather defensive. There's something in it, Hope. Something in it.'

'But what?' asked Hope. 'It's a natural phenomenon. You go down and you hear the sound. What if you hear it as voices?'

'Why do they all hear it as voices? Children's voices. I mean, if I go down and I hear the sound, and I say, 'Oh, it sounds a bit like a whimpering dog,' you'd tell me it sounds a bit like a cat. Big deal. That, to me, sounds normal, but they're all fighting off this idea of children's voices. Even a staunch Presbyterian woman from Harris is lying to me.' With that, he turned back to the window and started chuntering under his breath. 'Children's voices coming back to them.'

Chapter 12

Ross sat in the passenger seat of a nippy sports car which was hurtling down the side of Loch Ness. His partner, DS Urquhart, was always eccentric, but when she was in her car, it took on another level. The scarf she was prone to wear was blowing out behind her. She had a smart pair of driving goggles on as well, and her hair, usually so neatly kept, had been allowed its freedom and was also blowing behind her. The image was one that fascinated Ross, but what scared him was the driving. Clarissa Urquhart was a consummate driver, but she was happy to take small gaps in her stride, gaps that Ross would never have gone for.

'It's all about the engine you have, control of the car,' said Clarissa smiling broadly as the car continued on its merry way. 'You're used to these modern cars, they're a bit more sluggish than this. This has an elegance about it. It has style. This is no family hatchback horse.'

After visiting the bank manager, the pair of them had worked hard in trying to track down the owner of Smart Construction, but when they'd called the office, they had got nothing. A trace through business details showed that the company had been wound up. Ross had found an address in the Oban amongst the paperwork. They tried to make a call there but had no luck, and with the storm that had come through the previous night, they decided not to involve the local police in making a check. Instead, as the storm was blowing out the following morning, Clarissa decided they should pay a visit, just in case there was something untoward and the man might do a runner.

They arrived in Oban during the late morning, several heads turning at this nippy car that spun around the estate before parking up in front of a modern house. From the outside, Ross would've said it was a four or five-bedroom, but there was no car in the drive. However, there was a neat lawn that suggested someone was taking care of it. Together, the partners made their way to the front door and rang an elaborate doorbell they could hear reverberating around the house. There was no response, so Clarissa made her way to the front window.

'There's nothing in here, Als. The usual family home sofa, telly, some pictures on the wall. Nobody about though, no lights on.'

'I'll take a spin around the back,' said Ross. He departed down the driveway, peeking in first at the rear door and seeing an empty kitchen, before opening a gate into the extensive back garden. There were numerous trees, a shed, and a little river running through the back. As Ross made his way to the rear windows and looked in, he heard a shout from down the garden.

'Can I help you?'

Ross turned around and looked down towards a man waving. 'Yes, it's DC Ross.'

The man held his hand up to his ears and Ross shouted louder, 'It's DC Ross.' Again, the man shook his head, then put it down and started walking the fifty meters up to Ross.

On arrival, the man stood in front of Ross, put a hand down and lifted Ross's chin up, and gave a questioning face. 'It's DC Ross.'

'Sorry,' said the man, 'I'm deaf. I'm reading your lips, DC Ross.'

Ross nodded. The man's English was excellent, but there was that slight slur that gave away that he had never heard others speak.

'Sorry to bother you,' said Ross, 'I'm looking for Mr. Smart.'

'Mr. Smart's not here,' said the man. 'I think Mr. Smart's gone away.'

'Away?' asked Ross. 'Where?'

'Something about an opportunity in Canada. His secretary came here and told me. "Off to acquire new business"—That's what she said. She said I was to give an address to anyone if I met them'

'But he's coming back,' said Ross. 'You're still here doing the garden.'

'I don't know when he's coming, or if he's coming.'

'So why are you doing the garden?' asked Ross.

'I was paid by direct debit and it keeps coming in, so I come and do the garden. I've had no word from him. Nobody has told me what to do. I have never seen the secretary again.'

Ross held up a finger, walked around to the side of the house, and shouted for Clarissa Urquhart to come round.

When she joined them, Ross explained that the man was deaf. Clarissa stood in front of him watching closely as Ross continued to question him. 'This secretary, had you ever seen her before?'

'No,' said the man, 'But I have never seen anybody except Mr. Smart and once that Janey, his daughter.'

'She runs a retirement home now.'

'I don't know anything about that,' he said. 'But I do know that he was ready to throw her out. She was into drinking, drugs, and everything. "Squandering his money," he said. I saw their house. He used to think I was deaf so I wouldn't pick up on what was being said. They were pretty open in front of me when they had their house, but I could see their lips at times. It was all about drugs and drink, but he didn't like that. He didn't want that image.'

'She's taken over a retirement home,' said Ross.

'I think that might be because he wanted her to make something decent of her life. He was a good man, a family man before his wife died.'

'How long have you worked here for?'

'Eight years, but then she got cancer, and then Janey went off the rails. I know he was away to Eigg for a long time back and forward, and then after that, he went to Canada.'

'Have you got the address in Canada?' asked Ross.

'No, I got told it, but I couldn't remember it. She never wrote it down for me. The neighbour might have it. She visited everybody that day. Made sure everyone knew.'

'Okay,' said Ross, 'What's your name?'

'Andrew, Andrew Salt.' Ross took the man's details down, thanked him, and together with Clarissa, they made their way next door. After ringing the doorbell, it was answered by an elderly man in a cream coloured sweater. He looked delighted to have company.

'Hello, what can I do for you?'

'I'm DS Urquhart and this is DC Ross,' said Clarissa holding up her badge and warrant card, 'Can we ask you a few questions?'

'Certainly,' said the man. 'Just watching a bit of TV, but yes, certainly, break up my day.'

'It's about Mr. Smart next door.'

'Won't you come in?' and the man almost swept Clarissa in with an arm around her.

'Okay,' said Clarissa and made her way through into the man's living room. 'Take a seat, take a seat,' he said. 'Tea, coffee?'

'I don't think that's required,' said Clarissa and Ross noted the man's favourable eye towards her. In truth, he thought she spotted it as well, but being Clarissa, she would play it to get what information she required from the man. 'We're here to talk about your neighbour, Mr. Smart.'

'Oh, you won't find him,' said the man, 'He's gone to Canada.'

'So we've heard,' said Ross, 'How did you know that?'

'Well, it was all a bit sudden,' said the man. 'It appeared that his secretary came round; she said where he'd gone. I received a few postcards after that. It was a bit unusual because, to be honest, yes, I knew Mr. Smart, but we didn't talk a lot. Just did the usual neighbour thing of "hi" when you went out, but I got this letter about how well he was doing in Canada and the opportunities he's had.'

Clarissa leaned forward, smiling at the man, 'Do you think you could get me those postcards?'

'Oh, certainly,' said the man, 'just stay there. I won't be a tick,' and he disappeared out of the room.

'Sounds a little bit strange,' said Ross.

'Sounds very strange,' said Clarissa, and stood up, awaiting the man's return. When he came back in with his postcards, Clarissa took them off him, and carefully read each of them with her half-moon spectacles.

104

'It seems he's doing well,' said Clarissa. 'Made another business for himself. That was quick.'

'Sounded quick to me,' said the man. 'Sounds more like a brag and a boast. Don't know if any of it is true.'

'Thank you for this,' said Clarissa. 'Do you mind if I take these?'

'Not at all,' said the man, 'as long as you drop them back to me.'

'I'll make sure of that,' said Clarissa.

'Are you sure you won't stay for a cup of tea?' asked the man.

'Apologies,' said Clarissa, 'I am a busy woman, maybe next time.' She gave a graceful smile and walked out the door. Ross noted the man hardly paid him any attention when he left the room afterwards.

'This all seems a bit funny, Als,' Clarissa said outside.

'Does sound like a put-up job to me. Should we get the address then, get it checked out by the Canadians?'

'Yes,' said Clarissa. 'Let's do that.' She made her way back to the car before picking up her mobile phone. It took a good half an hour to work out what number to call, but she managed to get a police department in Canada and put a request in to have the building at the address checked out. Unbeknown to Clarissa or Ross, the building was up in the Yukon. Clarissa was surprised when she received a call from the Canadian Mounted Police almost an hour later just as they were finishing their lunch.

'This is DS Urquhart,' said Clarissa.

'This is Sergeant Anderson. Good day to you, ma'am. Just checking in from a request that you put through. That old shack up by Dawson, is that correct?'

'Why, yes,' said Clarissa. 'That's wonderfully quick of you.'

'No, it's fine, it's just outside the village here. I'm afraid that shack's been deserted. It has been for a long time. Although I did notice that there were several letters inside. The door wasn't locked, so I did have a look at them. Some seemed to be postcards, one or two formal type letters.'

'I'd appreciate any copies of them you could send over to us,' said Clarissa and gave an email address.

'That's not a problem,' said her Canadian colleague, 'but I notice one of them was from a place called Oban. It's like a postcard. It seems it's from the man's neighbour. It's addressed to a Mr. Smart, is that what you're looking for?'

'It is.'

'I did a bit of check with the Immigration Bureau and we haven't had anybody come in under that name to this address. Are you sure he made it over here?'

'I'm not sure of anything,' said Clarissa. 'We're just following up something that seems to be a little odd.'

'I'm sorry I couldn't be any further use to you, but your address is just a shack. Those are the letters in it and nobody around here has ever heard of the man or known anybody to be in that shack for over two years now. The only person that's been close to it has been the postie.'

'That's interesting,' said Clarissa, 'very interesting, but thank you for your time. It must be early in the morning for you.'

'I'm just finishing up off night shift. It gave me something to do. Glad I've been of help.'

Clarissa put the phone down and Ross noticed her smile. 'Any use?' he asked.

'Oh, yes, a lot of use. An empty shack, nobody of that name been in the area for over two years. The only person been near the shack is the postie. Somebody sold one here, Ross, somebody really sold one. Go back and see if we can get a better description of this secretary, from our deaf friend and the neighbour and let's see what we come up with.'

'Okay, well, it's somewhere to go, but it's not justifying that smile on your face.'

'No, but I spoke to a Mountie. I spoke to a proper Mountie,' said Clarissa, and Ross watched as she seemed to drift off in her mind somewhere else.

Chapter 13

Macleod stood outside the home looking out to sea, watching the orange boat as it made its way back and forth across what was still choppy water. Overhead, he could see the helicopter following a similar type of pattern, but in a perpendicular direction, above the lifeboat.

'How optimistic are the coastguard?' asked Macleod.

'Well, they've managed to land some of their teams over here as well, so they're searching the coastline, but in all honesty, Seoras, there's not much hope, is there? She'd have been out all night in that storm. If she'd been able, she'd likely have found shelter and be making her way back by now. Given all that's gone on before.'

'Given all that's gone on before, Hope? I'm not buying that. How many people can fall off a cliff, even if they are leaning over, even if they are down on the sand, even if they are going out in the most ridiculous of weather? Something's up here. I'm willing to call the search off.'

'Well, they say they're going to keep going until nightfall tonight, then they'll have a discussion, talk about whether it's worth pursuing, see the ground they've covered.'

'Okay,' said Macleod. 'I better go inside and see my other guests.'

The Inspector had requested that Janey Smart bring the rest of the local workers up to the house that evening for an interview with himself, and she'd arranged a room for him to interview each of them personally. The first had just arrived and he was taking a quick update from Hope before beginning that interview. Making his way inside, Macleod located the small room to find a man inside, who seemed rather edgy.

'Hello, I believe you're John McClintock?'

'That's right. I'm the chef here. Who are you?'

'Detective Inspector Macleod, investigating the deaths of the three residents.'

'Given the circumstances, I thought you would have described them as missing?' said John.

'Given the time involved, sir, I believe it's not an unreasonable assumption to assume they're dead.'

The man nodded. 'Well, I've got some things on in the oven, so I'm hoping this won't take that long. Obviously I'm at your disposal, Inspector, but just be aware, I do have other things I might need to keep an eye on in the kitchen. These people will still want fed no matter what happens.'

'I won't keep you very long.'

The interview with John was a quick one. The man could tell you everything about the residents' desires for food but he rarely engaged with them, remaining in the kitchen, bringing the food out, and then returning. As he said, he wasn't a personable man, and Macleod found that, although courteous, he was quick in everything he did, looking to get away. Macleod could understand that sort of person, but nonetheless, he went through all of his questions, finding that John knew very little about the people he served his food to.

Another interview followed with Angus the gardener, a similar man, or maybe this was an island trait. Someone who kept to his own business, out here away from the rest of the world. Following that, a young girl came in, possibly still a teenager, and Macleod watched how nervous she was as she sat down opposite him.

'Your name is Sarah Niles; is that correct?'

'That's correct, Inspector. I do the hairdressing up here.'

'How often are you up, Sarah?'

'Oh, maybe five times a week. Not for long, it just depends on what's needed. They like to have their hair brushed and set. It's not often I'm up cutting or that.'

'That's fine. I take it that you're quite chatty with the residents then?'

The girl looked a bit sheepish before she nodded.

'I'm not asking you to tell me anything private,' said Macleod, 'but I would appreciate answers to some questions I have. Do any of the residents talk about the sands?'

'The sands, Inspector? You mean the singing sands?'

'Exactly.'

'They don't just talk about it, they're on about it all the time to me, all about the noises that seem to come.'

'The noises?' queried Macleod. 'Can you expand on that?'

'Well, it's like this. I've lived here for the best part of my life, and I love the sands. You go out, you walk across them, it never ceases to amaze you. But we don't sit and talk about them back in the house or around the island. They are what they are. We know what they are; they're wonderful, but hey, they're normal to us. As much as these things ever become normal. They're not a talking point, is what I'm trying to say.'

'That's different for the residents,' said Macleod.

'Totally, I would say every time I'm doing their hair, the sands come up at some point.'

'Did they ever talk about children in association with the sands?'

'Not always children, Inspector. Sometimes they'll say to me, "Oh, you can hear it, you can hear voices." A few times I've heard them say children's voices. There was one time Angusina said to me, and she doesn't say a lot for she is the quietest of them—she said to me, "Can you ever hear them?" I said, "What? Hear who?" She said, "The children. Do you hear children down at the sands?" Of course, I said no, but then she said to me that she did, like they were calling her. Well, you know how it is, Inspector. Sometimes you do these old age pensioner places and you think some of them are a bit senile, not quite there, you just take it as that, don't you?'

'But you say every single one of them has done this?'

'They all have an obsession with the sands. Whether it's because they came here, it's in the title of the place, or what. I mean, it was a major attraction I believe when they put brochures out to try to attract people here. And it is unusual. We're only one of what, seven, eight sites in the world, I think? Could be wrong on that, but it is rare.'

'Do any of the islanders, Sarah, ever talk about hearing children's voices from the sands?'

'No, they don't even talk about them being voices. Yes, it's like singing, but in the sense that it's musical. That sort of floating-on-the-wind-type feeling, not voices of people talking.'

Macleod thanked the girl for her candour and then saw Alan, who ran the supplies for the home, a general dogsbody around the place. The man could only be in his thirties and he shook Macleod's hand furiously before sitting down, looking somewhat nervous.

'It's okay, sir, I'm not investigating you. I'm just looking for some general impressions of the place.'

'Impressions? What do you mean?' asked Alan. He was sitting in a boiler suit, his hair unkempt, and Macleod could see oil streaked across the back of his hands.

'I just wanted to know if you ever heard anything from the residents about the sands and voices?'

'I don't listen to them. I got cornered once by that Angusina. Oh, hellfire, damnation, and all the rest, mate. After that, I didn't talk to them. They don't bother me unless the radiator's not working or something like that, and I don't bother them. We get on great.'

Macleod quickly realised what a waste of time the interview would be and didn't delay the man, instead then speaking to Moira, who Janey Smart described as a counsellor and a nurse.

'I was wondering,' asked Macleod, 'are you aware of the residents' talk of voices at the singing sands?'

The black-haired woman shook her hair out behind her and gave Macleod an air of annoyance. 'You shouldn't read too much into these things. These people are elderly, old. There's only themselves here on an island. It's not the best place to be. Yes, they're in a community, but together, so there are little things that go wrong in their minds. They seem to congregate together.'

'What do you mean by that?' asked Macleod.

'Well, someone's senility grows legs because the other one hears of it. They then begin to fantasise on it. Very soon we've got a beach that's coming to life with children. There's nothing in it. Just that loss of the mind.'

'I have to be honest,' said Macleod. 'I find most of them to be very lucid. Certainly not senile. Yes, some of them are frail, but some of them are as strong as me.'

'Well, you're not exactly in the prime of life, are you, Inspector?'

Macleod took great offence but said nothing. If she started accusing him of being senile, he thought he might just go over the table after her. One thing that did strike him as bizarre was the fact that the woman wasn't using very technical terms, if she was indeed a qualified counsellor.

'Have they any other strange foibles I should know about?' asked Macleod.

'I wouldn't say so. Certainly, none that I would see as being relevant. You understand I can't tell you something unless it's got some relevance to your investigation. Patient confidentiality.'

'Of course,' said Macleod. 'But do you see anything else that you think could contribute towards the disappearances?'

'I don't know. Are they truly happy here? Who spends this sort of money to come here? It's a rather bizarre life. Especially at the end of their days.'

'I don't know,' said Macleod. 'There seems to be plenty of other people here on this island. They seem to enjoy what they're getting.'

'Most of them are not old,' said Moira.

'Did you live here before then?' asked Macleod.

'No. Answered an ad. I don't think Janey could find anyone here of a suitable calibre. She needed someone who could deal with the mental health of the residents and their physical needs as well. Obviously, someone who could recognise the need for a transfer, send them off to hospital. Job came up, I applied. I'm here.'

'I assume you're not enjoying it that much, then,' said Macleod.

'To be honest, not particularly. If I have my way, I'll probably be out of here in a couple of months, but please don't tell Janey. She doesn't like a lack of commitment.'

Macleod nodded. After asking the woman about the various routines of the residents, he decided to leave it for the moment. He did briefly ask what sort of things she discussed in her counselling sessions, but got a very firm rebuke telling him that that was patient confidentiality. Macleod wondered whether he should investigate this further. After all, she was dealing with the minds of people who were apparently launching themselves off a cliff. She didn't seem to be doing it very well. But he decided to save that for later, because if these were suicides, how could he prevent it? He was more bothered that they were actual murders.

There was one last person to see who went by the name of Cherry and was a person that Macleod thought he would struggle with. She had all the trappings of a new-age practitioner. As she appeared, with several earrings and large baggy clothes, Macleod fought his prejudices to give her a welcoming smile and a shake of the hand.

'What is it you do here exactly, Cherry?'

'Well, Inspector, it's head massage, muscle treatments, homeopathy. I use nature and I use various ancient techniques to try and give them wellness.'

'They all seem open to this?' asked Macleod.

'I can hear the scepticism in your voice, Inspector. I know they're not all open to it. Angusina specifically, but she is from a very narrow background.'

'She's from my background,' said Macleod. 'Yes, it may be narrow, but maybe there's wisdom in not engaging in everything under the sun.'

'Well, each to their own, Inspector. I think you'll find what I do for them is nothing strange. I'm simply trying to relax them, trying to get them to make full use of their muscles and legs. You've got to keep the body in some shape. Even as you get older.'

'As you say, each to their own. Let's talk about something slightly different. When you're with them, Cherry, do they ever speak about the sands?'

'They speak about the sands and then never shut up about the sands. To be frank, it's getting quite dull now. At first, I was interested. The whole nature side, I thought they were reaching out on some spiritual level. But the more and more I go through with it, it just seems like they're senile. Or at least that's what I thought of at first.'

'What do you mean at first?' asked Macleod.

'Well, you see, Inspector, they come and they tell you, "Oh, the sands are talking. There's voices, there's kids," and you think, "Yeah, yeah, here we go." And then I said, I thought, "Well, hang on, maybe they're right." So I talked through with them about it. What they heard, what it was like, and they keep talking about children.'

'Yes. They told a lot of people that they heard children. But when I talk to the residents about it, they won't tell me. They say so very little.'

'That may be because it's the death of a large group of children.'

Macleod suddenly sat up in his seat. 'How do you know

that?'

'They told me. One of the things I do is the massage, and that relaxes people, but also relaxes the mind. I think it lets their guard down.'

'They tell you anything about this death? How it happened, where?'

'Very little, but it's always a group of children, and they've always left them behind. That's the weird thing. This is consistent the whole way through.'

'When I spoke to Moira, she said it was like a shared fantasy. She believed it was coming from their senility.'

'Inspector, have you spoken to the people here?'

'Of course, I've interviewed them all.'

'How many would you say were senile?'

'I haven't any evidence of any them being senile.'

'No. Exactly,' said Cherry. 'This is a shared experience. I feel that.'

Macleod, despite his reservations about Cherry, was feeling that himself. 'But they never tell you where and when?'

'No,' said Cherry. 'But I get the feeling it's from a long time ago.'

'Why's that?' asked Macleod.

'Because they're never actually doing anything with the children, and they're cut down.'

'Cut down?' said Macleod.

'Yes,' said Cherry, 'with a machete. They mention the word machete.'

Chapter 14

The calm of the day had passed. Now late in the evening, the wind was picking up again. Hope stared out at the sea, watching the churning waves that once again brought back visions of her aunt being tossed here and there like a piece of flotsam at the mercy of the waves. She shivered involuntarily, thinking about it and at the thought of the aunt's arm separating, drifting off on its own. This sort of thing didn't happen to Hope when investigating murder cases. She could see as many bodies as she wanted and yet each time, she had no nightmares, no visions of the gruesome scenes she had seen. Instead, she'd always slept well.

Right now, she wanted to be with her lover, the Car-Hire-Man as the team teased her. She'd always seen herself being involved with someone dramatic but maybe this was what she needed, somebody stable who could appreciate her and wasn't looking out for their own ego. The one time she'd told her aunt about him, she had seemed pleased. She knew her aunt had her own issues with men, struggling with relationships as much as Hope had.

Hope heard someone behind her and turned to see Angusina.

The woman was dressed in a checked skirt with a grey jumper on top, and she carried a book in one arm. Hope smiled across but the woman merely stared passively at her before making her way over to a seat in the far corner. There she sat down, opened her book and began to read, ignoring Hope completely. As Hope stood watching the woman, she heard more footsteps, and she turned to see Daniel, the tall Englishman, entering the room complete with a pair of binoculars. He made his way over and sat on a settee that was closest to the window that faced the path for the singing sands.

'It's not much of a night to go birdwatching,' said Hope.

The Englishman half-smiled, then walked over to her before holding his binoculars out in front of her.

'If you looked through these, you could see all the way up the path. In fact, possibly even out to sea.'

'It's quite dark though, isn't it?' said Hope.

'Well, sometimes you get the moon coming across, those clouds drift away, and you can see the choppiness of the water. You can also see shadows with it. You can see people moving. You might not know who they are, but you'd soon see them moving.'

'So, you're what? Coming out to do sentry duty?' asked Hope.

'Effectively,' said Daniel. 'It's not quite how I'd would put it, but I like to keep an eye on our people. We're losing too many of them.'

'Well, you're not wrong there,' said Hope, 'but surely just stay here. Everyone that's gone out, it's saying that they booked before going. They've checked themselves out of the building.'

'I used to say that's going to be the case for all of them, but now I don't believe it. No, I'll stay here, and I'll keep my eyes trained.'

'How long for?' asked Hope.

'As long as necessary,' said Daniel.

Hope almost laughed. 'What happens next month or the month after that? In fact, what happens in twelve hours' time and you get hungry? Is somebody going to come and take over from you?'

'Are you mocking me?' asked Daniel.

'No,' said Hope, 'not in the slightest. I'm just pointing out the difficulties of this idea of having a permanent watch. You can't do it alone. If people are going to go and do things, they will find a way to do it if it is suicide.'

'You think there's something else at play, don't you?'

'It's hard to believe,' said Hope, 'a group of complete strangers in a residence home for a couple of months and the next thing they're all jumping off a cliff. No, it just seems too coincidental to be suicide.'

'Well, you're the detective,' said Daniel. 'I'm just the observer and I'm doing my bit. Call it a neighbourhood watch.' Hope smiled at him and asked if the man wanted coffee, but he put his hands up, waving Hope away, announcing he would get it instead.

'Angusina,' said Hope, 'why don't you help Daniel out? You could man the binoculars after an hour or so, give him a break.'

'What will be will be. If people want to take their life in that way, they deserve all that's coming to them.'

Hope felt the slur for her aunt and a fire ignited. She wanted to grab hold of the woman for such an insensitive comment. Her aunt wasn't like that.

'That's a bit harsh, don't you think?' said Hope, using as much restraint that she could muster.

119

'No, no,' said Daniel from across the room, 'there's no need for that. Here, here's some coffee,' and the Englishman walked back, handing Hope a steaming cup.

'You're too kind,' said Hope. 'I think I'm going to turn in for the night. Don't stay up too late.'

'I told you,' said Daniel, 'I'm here for the evening right through to the morning till somebody else comes. Got to keep an eye.' Hope nodded and smiled at the man before taking a quick look at Angusina. There was a scowl across Hope's face but when the woman looked up, she'd quickly changed it into a broad grin. Hope thought that Macleod must've had such difficulty growing up amongst these sorts of people. It was no wonder he turned out the way he had. As she stepped away, she heard a shout from the far end of the room.

'Stop. Don't go,' said Daniel.

'Why?' said Hope. 'What's up?'

'I don't know. Just don't go yet. Don't go. I can see something.'

'What do you mean you can see something? It's dark out there.'

'No, there was a . . . a cloud moved. There was definitely light there, I saw something in the surf. Something moving.'

Hope's shoulders sunk. This would be some fool's errand, surely, but you couldn't be too sure. After all, they'd already had numerous deaths. She'd have to go and check; there was no option.

'Whereabouts is it?' asked Hope.

'Off of the beach, off of the singing sands beach where the tide crashes in. It's not that far round from the path.'

'I'll get my coat. Just don't take your eyes off it,' said Hope.

'I can't see it anymore; it was there briefly.'

'Then what was it?' asked Hope.

'Something red, definitely something red.'

Hope's heart skipped a beat. Nancy was wearing red when she went. Was it she? Hope ran to the cloakroom at the front of the building, grabbed her jacket, then reaching around to tie her hair up lest it get buffeted round in her face by the wind, she came back to Daniel.

'You'll need more than that,' said Daniel. 'It's getting wild out there.'

Hope looked down at her jeans and her leather jacket that was now wrapped around her. 'It'll do for the minute. We may not have time if you're right.' With that, she made for the rear door.

'Hold on a second,' said Daniel, and he disappeared off before returning thirty seconds later with a large coat on. It had fluorescent stripes across the back. Hope turned around to Angusina who was still engrossed in her book.

'Angusina, if Janey's still there, go and get her and look for my boss. He'll be in the building somewhere. Check the guestrooms if you have to. Tell Macleod I need him.'

'Wouldn't dare; a woman ordering a man about,' said Angusina, but Hope shook her head. It was like the woman was delusional.

'Come on, Daniel. Let's go.' With that, Hope stepped out of the door and felt the full force of the wind hit her in the face. It was raining. Not as bad as the previous night, but what there was, drove into her face, and she put her hand up as she stepped out along the path. She turned several times to make sure Daniel was still with her. When they got close to the beach, she stopped, looking out towards the sea.

'I can't see anything,' she shouted over the wind.

'Just a moment,' said Daniel. 'I'll look through the binoculars. Just a moment. It's there,' he shouted and pointed out beyond the beach.

'Come on then,' said Hope, and together the pair made their way down onto the sand. Once again, the sound of the beach was being enveloped by the wind and Hope made her way right to the edge of the water.

'It was just over from here.' Daniel put his binoculars up to his eyes again. 'Yes, it's right there. It's a coat—yes, it's red. It's a coat and it's got . . . Oh, bloody hell. There's something inside it.'

'What?' asked Hope.

'That looks like a body. That looks like a—'

Hope threw off her leather jacket and strolled out into the water.

'Don't be daft,' said Daniel. 'It's not safe right there.'

'She's only fifty yards out. I can't risk leaving her; you don't know she's dead,' said Hope. 'We have to go for it.'

'No, we don't,' said Daniel. 'Get back, get back.'

Hope ignored him, and having tossed her mobile behind her, she dived into the water, swimming as hard as she could before lifting herself up for air. She looked around. There in the distance was a coat. Again, she struck out, her arms pulling her through the water, but she felt her body being thrown up by the swell of the waves. A second time, she lifted her head up, scanned the sea before fixing on an item that could possibly be red. It was so dark now, hard to tell true colours, but there was definitely an item over there.

Hope got close, reached out with a hand and grabbed something. It was Nancy, but her face was white and the eyes were motionless. Something inside Hope suddenly jumped.

Ignoring her feelings, she kept hold of the coat with one hand and tried to start swimming back with the other, but the tide kept pulling her out. She could feel herself beginning to tire. As hard as she kicked with her legs, she couldn't get the body to start moving inwards towards the land.

'Hope, Hope, get in here. Just let it go. Get in here.' It was Macleod's voice above the waves. He sounded hoarse, almost screaming. As she lifted her head up, she saw arms beckoning her, encouraging her to swim back. But this would be evidence. This may even help solve what was going on. She had to do it.

'Hope, just get back in. Let it go.'

She put her arm out again, pulling as hard as she could. Then she put her feet around the body, flexing her legs under its arms so she could pull with both her own arms, but the next time she looked up, the beach seemed further away. Her heart sank. She could feel a decision coming, and she knew which one she had to make. Her aunt was out here, fooling around somewhere, and if she wasn't careful, she could join her.

This time she struggled to get back up to the surface, and when she went back under, she half-swallowed the sea before choking. She let her feet slip away from the body, fought with her arms to get back up, broke into the air, and breathed deeply. She then began coughing and spluttering.

'Get back in. That's an order,' shouted Macleod. Hope allowed herself to float momentarily and sucked in long draughts of air. When she looked back again to the beach, she now was struggling to hear the voices through the wind, but she allowed herself to rotate, then began to swim, pulling with each stroke as hard as she could. It would be a race; she could fatigue before long if she didn't keep her pace up. She kept going, barely looking up, hoping she was striking in the right direction, and then she felt her arms go suddenly weak. Her legs didn't feel like they were kicking anymore. Was this it? Was she fatiguing properly?

She raised her head above the water, drew in a breath but didn't have time to look to see where she was before she suddenly went back underneath. Her breath went from her. She struggled to hold it, looking to go back up to the surface, but this time her arms would not carry her. Her breath went out through her mouth, through her nose, and she knew she could not suck in anymore.

A pair of arms suddenly picked her up by her armpits and dragged her out.

'Just stand up,' said Macleod, 'just stand.' Hope put her feet down and found she was in only five feet of water. A wave crashed onto her back and she stumbled forward and suddenly, the pair of them were under the water again, but Macleod was strong, lifting himself back up and hauling Hope as well.

'Keep walking. Keep walking. We're just off the beach. We're practically there. Keep walking.'

Every step felt like lead, but the arms of MacLeod were underneath, pulling her along, and then another voice appeared beside her, an English voice, and a second pair of arms were dragging Hope. They laid her down on the beach. On her back, she breathed in huge lungfuls of the cold night air. Her face was feeling the bitter wind and she began to shake before she felt another jacket being thrown over.

'We need to get you inside,' said Macleod, 'get you checked out. You can't stay here.'

'I had the coat, Seoras. I had her. That was Nancy. I had her red coat. I just couldn't. I just couldn't.'

'Stop talking,' said Macleod, 'just suck it in slowly. We're going to need to get you to your feet and help you back inside.' Hope looked up and saw the man shake. The cold was obviously bothering him as well as he stood in his long coat, which was dripping water like it had been held in a shower.

'Best get her up,' said Daniel. 'If we stay here, she'll go cold. She'll shiver.'

'And she'll get hypothermia,' said Macleod. 'I have done my training. Come on, Hope. Up on your feet, let's move.'

'But I had her. She's out there, Seoras.'

'She's with the sea and the sea has got her, and the sea is going to keep her because we're getting you inside. Now, that's an order. Get on your feet, Sergeant.' Hope turned over, raised herself onto her knees, but then struggled. An arm went under each armpit of her own, hauling her to her feet. The two men then helped her along, up the steps from the beach, onto the path back to the home. As they stepped in through the front door, leaving puddles behind from the dripping clothing and wet shoes, Hope collapsed onto a sofa and then before a desperate face appeared, an American accent asked her, 'Was Nancy there?'

'I had her,' said Hope. 'I almost had her.'

125

Chapter 15

'I hope you're wrapping up for the night, Als. I know Macleod expects results but there's no need to go into the wee hours for it.'

Alan Ross looked up from his computer, briefly nodded at his senior partner, and then put his head back down.

'I mean it, Als. You need to get home.'

'I'm coming, Clarissa, I'm coming, but wait. Come round here; look at this.'

Complete with her shawl already around her and a scarf across her neck, Clarissa stepped around and leaned over Al's shoulder, looking at the screen in front of her. She could see a picture of black people in what she believed to be Africa in a small village, what seemed like a relief camp.

'What am I looking at?'

'This is the Congo, 1960. This village was overrun by hostile forces, with no survivors. It went by the name of Delta Camp.'

'Well, that's interesting,' said Clarissa. 'But I'm really not seeing your fascination with this.'

'They wiped them out. All of them. The men, the women, and the children. Especially the children—it was brutal.'

'I'm as sad as anyone else is,' said Clarissa, 'but I still don't understand why I'm looking at this.'

'The residents of the care home, they're linked to this.' Clarissa stood up behind Ross, looked around the room to make sure no one else was there, and then turned back to him. 'Are you all right? I mean, like, are you being serious?'

'Completely,' said Ross. 'I'm being completely serious. Each one of the residents is attached to this camp.'

'How do you know that?'

'I looked into their histories. Looked for their work records all the way back. I had to do a lot of digging, but at some point, they all crossed into this camp. Some had been there for years before. No one is obviously there after, but there's also no particular record of them leaving. They start on their jobs, but nobody says anything about what happened before.'

'How do you mean?' asked Clarissa.

'Right,' said Ross. 'Let's start at the beginning, Joel Grimshaw. Joel Grimshaw was a water specialist sent by an aid agency to assist with the water sanitation within the camp. He's there for about a year beforehand. The people had been displaced, had come to this camp and there was nothing. Joel was responsible for making sure that they had clean water, place to do toilet, showers, et cetera, to be able to function as a makeshift village.'

'Okay,' said Clarissa. 'So, Joel was there, did some work. What else have you got?'

'Natalie Ferdinand. She was there as a nurse, particularly midwifery. She's there for about six months beforehand. You then have the Americans, Jake and Nancy Griffin. They've gone over as missionaries.'

'Missionaries? There's nothing in there saying about missionaries. There was Angusina, who the boss said was from

127

Harris, but came from the same background as him. Now, she could maybe be the missionary type.'

'You see, you're right there. She was, too, but you've got Jake and Nancy in there, working for two years there, even before the foundation of the camp within the country. Angusina comes in for the last three months.'

'Okay. So, Jake and Nancy are there as missionaries; you've got Angusina there as a missionary.'

'And also as a medical person,' said Ross. 'She wasn't just put in to spread the good news. Jake and Nancy were.'

'Okay. Who else have you got?'

'Daniel Edwards, the Englishman. He's there as a logistics expert.'

'Okay. But you've still got more people, haven't you, to tie in?'

'Yes. Georgie is there as a response from the Catholic Church. She's a nun.'

'Get away. A nun? From what Macleod told me about her, she didn't sound like a nun.'

'Well, she was, and apparently, a bit of tension between her and Angusina, from what notes I have of the camp.'

'But what about Dennis and Sheila? The couple from Glasgow who were the clothing gurus. I mean, you didn't have people out there clothing them, did we?'

'No, no. They're representing the empire. They're out there as people from the government. They were moving around, trying to make sure that assistance was being had. Quite low-level.'

'Okay. So you've fixed them all in the same place at the same time. That's going to be interesting for the boss. Which camp was this, you say?'

'It was referred to as Delta Camp. There were a number of different ones. Alpha, Beta, Charlie, Delta, Echo camps. The other camps eventually were dispersed. People moved on to find new homes. With Delta Camp, the record stops after saying it was overrun, but that's it. That's all it said about it. Hostile force, no survivors. But as far as I can see, all these people were working at Delta Camp.'

'So, you're wondering,' said Clarissa, 'why they're still here. What's the tale from here to there?'

'Exactly,' said Ross. 'That's exactly what I want to know. There was a military presence around at the time, small, low-key. I'm not sure they were at the camp, but they were in the area. Now, I managed to trace a Major Michael McGovern but he's now in an old folk's home, and apparently isn't too well. I'm going to go and see him tomorrow morning.'

'No, you're not,' said Clarissa, and saw Ross's shocked face. 'We're going to go and see him. I'm not missing this one.'

'I'm just trying to get my story straight. He could be difficult to talk to. Apparently, he comes and goes, from the conversation I had earlier on with the nursing home. We'll hopefully catch him in a good mood.'

'Well, the boss is enough of an old fossil. You should be experienced at that, Ross.'

Ross looked up at Clarissa, his face showing nothing.

'It's okay. He's not here, you can laugh.'

'What's your thing with the boss?' asked Ross. 'If I'm not out of line, what is it?'

'What do you mean?' asked Clarissa, as she pulled over a seat, leaving Ross to think he'd said something wrong.

'I'm not probing,' said Ross. 'I mean, it's okay. It's fine. I'm not saying anything is wrong here. I'm just—I get a little bit of tension between you and the boss all the time. I know he's a pain sometimes and he's quite grumpy and sharp, but you're always having a dig at him, the old bits and pieces.'

'Just keeping him on his toes. That's the trouble, you see. You guys, you're just so subservient to him. Macleod says this. There we go, not a problem. Take you, Ross. He's dumping all his work on you. You've got nobody with you to back it up. I mean, I'm as good as a chocolate teapot when it comes to all this computer stuff but you used to have Kirsten. Kirsten was the one working with you doing this, sharing the load. You need to be getting somebody out of uniform trained up on this. Somebody you can hand stuff down to.'

'When it gets busy, he does let them come through.'

'And does he ever promote them? Does he ever say, oh, Ross could deal with an extra person now? No, he has his little team firing things out to. He needs to take better care of you.'

'I'm okay,' said Ross. 'He's been good for me. We're quite highly thought of as a team.'

'No, you're not. It's Macleod that gets all the credit. Look at Hope. Smart cookie on the way up, but every time something comes in, he's the one that gets the credit for it because it's his group, his department.'

'But that's true of anywhere, isn't it?' said Ross.

'No, it's not. He needs to promote you guys more. I mean, bringing me in, what's the point of that?'

'Do you really want to know?' said Ross.

'Yes,' said Clarissa. 'I want to know.' Ross looked at her again, unsure if he should answer. 'Thing is, Hope's all action and that. She's clever too, but I think Macleod thinks that the old ways are a bit better. Thinks you can show her some of that. A bit of, I guess he'd call it, savvy.'

'Savvy, whoever calls it savvy? What you really mean is he wants her to know when you go against the rules, you break it and get it done.'

'Probably. I mean, it's not because of your fighting skills, is it? As much as you can handle yourself. Hope can handle herself too. She's a big girl. Strong, six feet. She could take me on any day.'

'Als, I'd take you on any day and I'm a woman who should be picking her pension up soon. You're too genteel, you're too nice. You're the epitome of what the middle class want the police to be. That classy detective who speaks politely and all posh, can operate computers well and solve things by detecting. I'm not. I'm the old school. Get in and shake it up a bit. Macleod can do that too. I bet his teeth come out when he's up against it.'

Ross sat back in his chair and put his arms behind his head. 'He does, you know. He does. Not afraid to take charge, but you're wrong about Hope. He trusts her implicitly. He's put her off under the radar, taking all the attention on himself to get the job done, and she's come up with the goods. I think you underestimate her.'

'If that's the case, why am I here?' said Clarissa. 'I'm not some newbie off uniform. Ask yourself that, Als. But for goodness' sake, shut that ruddy computer down, get off to bed. What time are we meeting in the morning?'

'Eight o'clock,' said Ross.

'Right, then, I'll be here with the car.'

'Should we take mine instead?' said Ross. 'Might rain.'

'You do realise the other reason I'm here.' Ross shook his head. 'It's to teach you a bit of style.'

The following morning, Ross parked his car on his way into

131

the office an hour before Clarissa was expected to arrive. He sat down in front of his laptop again, made himself a coffee, and ate his breakfast, staring over the reports of Delta Camp he'd unearthed. In his mind, he wondered if he'd get the credit for this. And he deserved it. Not many people would've linked through all the histories, found the one place in time. He'd been on the phone to different people, asking about previous employment. He'd even had to coax out from a Catholic priest the fact that Georgie had been there, although he was surprised when the man swore about her.

An hour later the door was flung open. Clarissa entered in a skirt that seemed to billow despite being inside the office and a snappy jacket with a brooch on the side.

'Good morning, Als. It's time to take in the fresh air.' Ross stood up and put on his coat.

'There's no need to be like that. Open top driving is the only way to go.' Clarissa strolled out of the room, hastily followed by an already shivering Ross.

The drive took just over an hour, and Ross located the quiet residential home located just above Aviemore. From the car park, he could look out at the mountains around and see why someone in their later years might see this as a place to be. The town was nearby, if they were indeed allowed out for day trips, but there was a serenity about the place, and even as the distant mountains had snow on the top of them, one could not deny the picturesque beauty around. However, Ross was feeling like his ears would fall off due to the cold wind that had assaulted them for the hour's drive to the home.

'Chin up, Als. Time to go to work,' said Clarissa, breezing to the front door and pressing the buzzer. 'Do you want to take charge here?' she said. 'It was your bag. You're the one that found this place. Maybe you should talk to the gentleman, use a bit of that quiet Ross resolve.'

'I'll talk to him if you want,' said Ross, 'but it's your call, you're the senior.'

'Well, I was telling Macleod last night, even though he wasn't in the office, he needs to let you people shine. It's all yours, Ross; it's all yours.'

The door opened and Ross introduced himself to a lady in green scrubs. She advised she was one of the cleaners and showed them into an office where a man in a smart suit welcomed them.

'DC Alan Ross, and this is DS Clarissa Urquhart. We're here to speak to Major Michael McGovern.'

'Ah, the major. Well, we'll see how he is today. Drifts in and out, that sort of thing, but you'll have to catch him at a good point. He's not a bad old soul. Can be a bit cantankerous if he's getting sleepy, but by all means. I think he's already up in the common room.'

The pair were led down a corridor and then into a room with a grand view back out across the car park and towards the mountains Ross had previously admired. There was a man sitting in a chair and as Ross got close to him, he saw he had striped pyjama bottoms on and was wrapped up in a robe, his grey hair failing to cover his head.

'Hello? Major?' said Ross, leaning beside him.

'Who the blazes are you? Have you got the coffee?'

'We can get you the coffee, Major,' said Ross. 'That's not a problem.'

'Her, that woman. Tell that filly to go and get me the coffee.'

Ross nearly burst out laughing when he saw Clarissa's shocked face. 'If you wouldn't mind, Sergeant, I think the

Major requires a coffee.' Clarissa looked indignant and she turned away, wagging her finger at Ross.

'They're not the best at looking after you in this place at times. Back in the day, we all had someone running to do these chores. They ran the canteen, these women. Excellent, top class.'

'Changed days,' said Ross. 'Changed days.'

'Indeed,' said the Major. 'You get some sort of whoopsie of a man in here now to do it. There's a guy comes in here, claims he's a nurse. Ridiculous. Back in my day, a nurse was a woman, not one of those men.'

Ross was not sure how to take the slur. The man was clearly from a bygone day and even though intimidation and even abuse still existed, he could tell the man operated when Ross's kind were not welcome.

'Major, do you remember Delta Camp?'

'Bloody awful show. Were you there?'

'No, Major, I wasn't there.'

'Where were you? Weren't at Charlie Camp, were you? You look like somebody from Charlie Camp.'

'Yes,' said Ross. 'Charlie Camp, but do you remember Delta Camp?'

'Yes. Terrible show. We weren't to know they were coming. If I had've known they were coming, we'd have been there. We'd have trounced the buggers, but they left nothing. You understand? They left nothing. Not a man, not a woman, not even a child. They left nothing.' The Major suddenly stared out at the window and Ross wondered what he was looking at. He could see tears suddenly running down the Major's face.

'I held him. I held him. Do you understand? Last one. Last one alive. So small. They must have forgot him, but he had injuries. Couldn't save him, but I held him till he died. He cried at first,' said the Major. 'Can't blame him though. Couldn't have been more than six months, but I held him. I was with him when he went; he didn't die alone. They can't die alone.'

Clarissa blundered in at that point with the coffee, putting it down beside the Major, who suddenly snapped back, looking up at her. 'Milk in it, two sugars.' Ross looked over and saw the black coffee.

'Just the way you like it, Major,' said Clarissa, and stepped back behind Ross. Ross saw the man take the cup, drink a bit, and chew it around his mouth before swallowing.

'Milk these days, it's not right. Can't get the stuff.'

'You were telling me about Delta Camp,' said Ross, 'holding the child. When did you go to it? When did you arrive?'

'We got there too late,' said the Major. 'Too late. We weren't told. If we had've been there straight away, we'd have stopped it. If they had've held it up, got word through, but those that knew didn't come. We found them later.'

'Who?' asked Ross.

'Don't know their names, but the white people, the workers, those who should have got the message to us. They ran off, hid. They knew they were coming, and they all died. I told them, I told them I held that child, and do you know what they said? "Who cares?" The lives weren't important.'

'Dear God,' said Clarissa. 'They just left them?'

'Yes,' said the Major, 'to die. They couldn't protect themselves. I could've, we would've.' The man's eyes were stained with tears, streaming down his chin, where occasional drops fell onto his dressing gown. 'We could have saved them.'

'Who were the white workers?' asked Ross. 'Can you tell me who any of them were?'

135

'Don't remember names. Don't remember them except one. One woman. Not much of a woman. She came from up north. She said to me, "God's Providence. We all trust in God's Providence." Do you know what I said to her? I took my weapon and I held it in her face. I told her, "I trust in this. I trust that this would've stopped it." I told her that God would damn her, and she told me not to take his name in vain. Too much. Too much, son. You understand?' The Major began to cry, weep uncontrollably, so much so that a nearby worker came over, putting her arm around him.

'I think you've upset him.'

'It wasn't us,' said Clarissa. 'Something from the past.'

'We have what we need,' said Ross. 'I won't disturb him any longer.' He reached forward and put his hand onto the Major's. He gripped it tight.

'Not my fault, son,' said the Major, 'not my fault. I held him till the little chest stopped beating. Not my fault.'

'It wasn't your fault,' said Ross, and he stood up and walked solemnly out of the building. When he reached Clarissa's car, he didn't get in, but stayed looking out towards the mountains.

'Poor man,' said Clarissa. 'Blaming himself for that.'

'Not his fault,' said Ross. 'He blames himself. Who blames them?'

Chapter 16

'Are you going to do something about this, Macleod? It's getting ridiculous.'

Macleod was standing in the entrance hall awaiting Janey Smart, and he narrowed his eyes as Georgie spat the comment towards him.

'As far as I'm aware, we don't have definitive proof that anyone was murdered. We have a suspicion, but I think I should suggest that everyone stays indoors, because the wind is getting up again. It's going to be another wild night.'

'That's it, is it? Is that the best you can come up with? I don't think you're wise. I don't think you're with it at all. A good detective would've stopped these things by now.'

Macleod wondered how, when people kept disappearing off to locations they shouldn't be in. Every time someone went out there, it seemed the person either died or spotted somebody in the water. Surely, one of the key things to staying alive was not to be out there.

'I've warned you all,' said Macleod, 'to not go out on that path. Stay in, lock your doors if you want to, but don't go outside.'

'Do you think I don't know that?' said Georgie. 'You won't catch me out there. You would be out of your mind if you went there. No, I'll be inside, Inspector Macleod. You can count on that.'

Macleod watched her shuffling off and turned to see Janey Smart arrive from her smaller house behind the township.

'Sorry to keep you waiting, Inspector. Do you want to come through to the office?'

'Absolutely,' said Macleod. 'How are you?'

'Oh, coping, Inspector. I mean, first, it's a tragedy what's been happening. There's also the pressure of the business, obviously, because who's going to want to come to a home where people keep committing suicide? If that's what's happening and your suspicions are incorrect.'

'I didn't say I had suspicions,' said Macleod. 'I just don't like unexplained circumstances.'

'Well, whatever. Part of running this home with the long-term investment is getting new people in. This doesn't help. It doesn't help me at all.'

Macleod could understand that. There was nothing within him believing that Janey Smart did anything untoward towards her residents. What would be the benefit? One could say bumping them off quick she would keep the money that they'd all paid upfront, but would you be able to fill the home again? You wouldn't do it this quickly, you would do it one at a time. Why in the same place? It made no sense whatsoever. If Macleod was going to kill off the residents, he'd do it with plausible accidents. Maybe an overdose. Something that said, 'I did this to myself,' but they were all talking about children coming home from the sands, the sands that were talking to them, taking leaps off the path into the sea. Something was seriously wrong here, but he didn't see Janey Smart as part of it.

'Would you like a coffee, Inspector, while we have a chat?'

'Absolutely,' said Macleod. 'You can feel a chill from that wind even when it's outside.'

'Well, it's warm in here and you are, of course, welcome as long as you need to be. It's black, isn't it?'

'Thank you,' said Macleod and walked past Janey's desk to look out of the window. The office was located at the corner of the building. When he looked left, he could see the car park at the front of the house. When he looked right, he could see the edge of the building on the start of the path up towards the singing sands.

'What is it about up there?' asked Macleod. 'Why go up there?'

'I guess it's the view, Inspector. I guess it's the mystique of the sands.'

Macleod gave a slight jump. He hadn't realised he'd asked the question out loud, but now he had, he thought he should continue.

'Why? What's the draw? Suicide comes from a depression normally, a circumstance forcing you towards it, as best I understand it. Either that or an automatic reaction to the brain you can't control. Something of that ilk. No one here seems that down, but they are talking of voices being heard.'

'It's all very mysterious. You'll be speaking of spirits next,' said Janey.

'No, I won't,' said Macleod. 'I don't go for that. No, there's something in this. There's a hand I'm not seeing.'

'Well, it's one I'm not seeing either,' said Janey. 'Here, black coffee as you like it.'

Macleod took the cup and stared back out of the window. He looked left again to the car park where he saw the rain pouring down and the drops hitting the cars and bouncing off the roof. He heard a crack of thunder and something inside him shivered. Glancing right, he saw a figure on the path. The coffee dropped from his hand, the cup shattering.

'Inspector, are you all right?' But Macleod was gone.

The Inspector shoved open the door of the office, running at full pelt back into the main corridor and then into the common room. In the corner, his eyes caught Angusina's head down in what seemed like prayer.

'Get my sergeant,' shouted Macleod. 'Get McGrath now.' He saw Angusina look up as Macleod sprinted for the door. 'Just get her.'

He reached the far door that led out to the singing sands path and opened it to be hit by a blast of cold air. His trousers became instantly soaked. His long coat had been left behind and he was in his suit jacket, but it wasn't long before he felt the water turning his shirt wet. Up ahead he could see a small figure, difficult to make out and the rapidly changing shadows, but when lightning lit up the sky, Macleod could see it was a small woman, and his initial reaction was to think it was Georgie.

'Stop,' shouted Macleod, but the wind took his voice, and he doubted the woman would have heard him. She was walking at a pace and, following her, Macleod thought he was making ground. If he could keep his legs pumping, he would arrive with her soon. He felt the gravel kicking out under his feet and wrapped his jacket around him as he ran, determined to keep as much water off him as possible. It ran down from his hair onto his face, and soon he could feel everything begin to drip to the floor.

'Georgie. Georgie, would you stop?' But the woman up ahead continued to walk. It didn't take long for her to reach the path round to the cliff at the top of the singing sands. By the time Macleod got within twenty yards of her, she had a hand on the rail and was looking over at the sea.

'Please, woman, would you stop?' Georgie looked around at Macleod and carefully, she lifted one leg over up onto the rail, and then another, sitting precariously over the edge.

Her face was blank and Macleod struggled to see emotion. Then her head turned slowly towards him in a way he found to be eerie.

'Can you hear the children, Inspector?' said Georgie. 'The wee voices. Can you hear the wee voices they used to sing? "Sing to me," I would tell them; "sing to me." You didn't get chocolate out there, Inspector. You got little treats, bits of this and that that you could feed them, and I did it. Trust me to bring them up to be good Catholic kids, not them Presbyterian ones. They'd sing with me. Do you like singing, Inspector?' Macleod walked forward. 'Don't, Inspector. I'm going to go, so you can just stay where you are.'

'Don't,' said Macleod, pulling up suddenly. 'I'll stay here. I'll not come closer, but you need to talk to me. You need to tell me about the children.'

'Tell you? Can you not see them? Look down at the sand, Inspector. They're all there on the left. He's seven, I think. Seven. I remember him from the school. I was never good with the names, but that didn't matter. That was the thing out there. Their language wasn't really the same, but yet we tried to teach them, teach them in English when they didn't speak much of it. Sounds like a stuff of nonsense, doesn't it? But

141

they're there. Can you hear them singing? They can sing in tune. Proper tune, not like we sing.'

Georgie stood up on the rail and Macleod went to move closer. 'No, Inspector. I've got this. I used to be in the ballet when I was young, before I took my vows.'

Macleod had expected her to stare at him, but she didn't. It was as if she was looking beyond him. Like she knew he was there, but only because he'd spoken.

'Come down, Georgie. Come down and speak to me.'

'I'm going to dance, Inspector. They like that. They thought it funny of me, a nun dancing. Can you imagine my wimple around me as well? I went swinging my head, dancing away. Must have been like a *Sound of Music* moment for them. That was the thing, Inspector. That was all gone. All that teaching was not worthwhile. I taught them nothing that could help them, nothing that could defend them. I should have taught them about warfare, the medieval ages, about trebuchets, and arrows, and bows, and swords. Maybe that might've done them some good. Swords against machetes, because you know what, Inspector?'

Macleod edged closer slowly as he saw the woman wasn't looking at him.

'Do you know what? I waved bye-bye to them. I waved bye-bye to them. I smiled. I smiled before the machetes. I couldn't do it to them. I couldn't do it to them. I couldn't let them see what I knew was coming.'

'Come down, Georgie,' said Macleod, now less than six feet from the woman.

'I waved bye-bye like this, Inspector.' Macleod saw her put her hand up and then turn towards the sea. 'And I'm coming. I'll come now for you.'

142

Macleod raced forward, threw his arms out, but the woman had left. He found himself hanging over the barrier, looking down as her body tumbled. He turned his head as the figure bounced awkwardly, and then splashed into the sea.

'Seoras,' shouted Hope, 'did she?

'Just jumped. Just jumped, Hope.' Macleod turned around and saw his sergeant sprinting for the steps down to the beach. He followed her and saw Janey Smart approaching.

'Get them all back inside that building,' shouted Macleod. 'Keep them there. Nobody leaves.'

He continued his descent down the steps and saw Hope treading out into the water. She reached out and grabbed Georgie's arm. The sea was not far in, and the woman had bounced off the rocks into a shallow area. Hope was dragging her up the beach and Macleod assisted until they were clear of the water, at which point, Hope leaned down whereas Macleod looked at the head. He saw it was so badly caved in that there was little chance of any life.

Hope pinched Georgie's mouth open and started to do CPR, but Macleod knew it was hopeless. After a few minutes, Hope looked at Seoras and he shook his head.

'She's gone. She's blooming gone,' said Macleod. He could feel tears streaming down his face. He'd been so close!

'It's not your fault, Seoras,' said Hope and put her arms around him, but he shrugged her off.

'I don't understand,' he said to Hope. 'I don't understand. She just told me up there that there was no way she'd come out on this path. She meant it. She meant it, Hope.'

'Why was she here?'

'The children. She was hearing the children. What did they do to them? She said they died.'

'It must have been guilt,' said Hope. 'But what children? I don't understand either, Seoras.'

Macleod looked down at the body. 'Come on,' he said, 'We'll need to get a bag. Get her out of here before the tide comes in and takes her.'

'Not your fault, Seoras,' said Hope.

'I know that,' said Macleod. 'I just don't know whose it is.'

Chapter 17

Macleod answered the phone still feeling a little bit weary from the night before. The time now in the later hours of the morning, he still felt uneasiness from the night's situation. Everything was starting to feel a little bit repetitive. Were they some sort of lemmings? What was the commonality between them all causing them to do this?

'Good morning, sir. It's Ross.'

'What did you come up with?' asked Macleod.

'Clarissa said I should speak to you because we've just come from a residential home.'

'I take that you haven't been having the issues we've been having.'

'Sir?'

'We lost another one last night. Jumped off in front of me.'

'Are you okay?'

'I'm fine, Ross. What do you want?'

'I was doing some digging, sir, and I went to see an old major in a retirement home. It turns out that all your residents were at some time at Delta Camp, a place in the Congo in the 1960s.'

'All together? Doing what?' asked Macleod.

'There were various paths to this situation. I'll start with Georgie, she was a nun. Angusina, effectively a Presbyterian missionary. We had people doing water sanitation. I'll send the whole list through on the email. What you need to know is Delta Camp was a refugee camp. There were some tribal issues and it appears that Delta Camp was overrun by hostile force with no survivors. The major I spoke to—he was with military in the area—said a group of white workers survived and they wandered into a nearby military camp one day, but has no idea how they survived.'

'Really, Ross? You are telling me all these residents were together when a village of African people were killed and they walked out? Do you know what happened to them?'

'No,' said Ross. 'I don't.'

'Well, I'm going to find out. I'm pulling them all in together. What was the major's name?'

'Major Michael McGovern. A little bit challenged mentally these days, but the tears he was crying were real when he talked about the camp, about a massacre, sir—men, women and children.'

The word rang out loud with Macleod. The children were calling, coming back to them. Was this what it was about? But how? Some sort of mass hysteria?

'Good work, Ross. I'll hear more from you, but in the meantime, Clarissa and yourself send through the details, see if we can flesh them out more. While you do that, I'm pulling everyone in here together. I'm going to confront them with this.'

'Very good, sir,' said Ross. 'Are you okay?'

'Ross, I'm fine. It's not the first person I've seen jump in front of me.'

'No, sir. It's not. One of them must get to you at some point.'

'Sorry, Ross. You're just doing what you should do. I'm okay. I'm just getting on with it. To tell you the truth, Alan, I want to get back off this island. I need to get to the bottom of this and fast. It feels like I've got a load of lemmings, all ready to jump off the cliff.'

'It's a bit odd though. Isn't it?' said Ross. 'I mean, if they went through bad history and they were all committing suicide, taking their own lives for an action they did or didn't do, you can understand it, but all gathered together at the same time, you don't do it as a group. They do it one by one. Are they egging each other on? I'm sorry, Inspector, but it's not making sense.'

'Not yet it's not, Ross. It will do.'

Macleod closed down the call and looked for Hope. He found her staring out the window at the wild weather outside.

'Round them all up, Hope.'

'All of them?' said Hope. 'You mean the residents?'

'Yes, the residents. All of them. Get them in here. We need to have a word.'

'What's happened,' asked Hope. Macleod explained the details that Ross had sent through. 'He's sending more in the email, but I've got enough to attack them with. They've been keeping stuff back from us. They all knew each other from the sixties.'

'Okay, Seoras. I'll bring them in. In the common room there at the front, is that where you want them?'

'Yes. Just make sure they've got a view of the singing sands. We'll find out what on earth they're on about.'

It took Hope twenty minutes to round everyone up and

gather them together. During this time, Macleod made himself a coffee and gathered his thoughts together. He stood in the middle of the room, as Hope brought them through, arranging them in a circle around the Inspector. He drunk the last of his coffee, watching them all closely before placing it on a table at the side. He then strolled back into the centre of the room.

'Would any one of you like to tell me about the Congo in 1960?' His eyes flicked from person to person looking for a reaction, but they were remarkably measured.

'No idea what you're talking about, Inspector,' said Daniel. 'The Congo? I know some of us have been out in Africa in different places, but I don't think anyone's ever mentioned the Congo.'

Macleod stood up to the tall Englishman, putting his face directly in front of him. 'The Congo, sir. Tell me about the Congo in 1960.'

'No idea what you're talking about, Inspector,' said a voice behind him. He turned and saw Sheila, decked out in some in some remarkable clothing. 'You must be off your head.'

'I wish I was. I really do, but you see, Joel Grimshaw was a water specialist out there. A year before, he arrived. Natalie was out there as a nurse. Jake, you and Nancy went out there as missionaries, didn't you?' Jake looked up. Macleod could see tears coming from his eyes. 'You, Mr. Edwards, you ran logistics out there. Stop lying and tell me about the Congo.'

Macleod watched Daniel look at his fellow residents and then his head slumped. 'Okay. We were there. We were all out in the Congo together, but we didn't know each other before we went, all doing different jobs.

'But you all ended up working at Delta camp. Didn't you?'

'That's correct,' said Sheila. 'There were five camps people were posted to. We ended up at Delta camp, all of us. You have to understand, Inspector, it was a rough situation. There was civil unrest, and we were just there to help people. Try and make things better.'

'What happened?'

'What do you mean what happened?' asked Daniel. 'Not much, but we were all rather surprised when we got here and saw everyone again. Of course, a lot of us have changed, but once we heard the voice, and once we saw some of the eyes, well, we knew who each other was.'

'And that didn't strike you as suspicious?'

'It seemed like a very happy accident,' said Daniel. 'Out there, we got on okay.'

Macleod spun around, searching faces, but they were resolute and nodding, except for Jake, who still had tears.

'What about you, Jake?'

'It was happy times for me and Nancy,' said Jake. 'We did some good work for the Lord.'

Macleod looked over at Angusina, sitting in her plain grey skirt and white jumper. He could see her shoulders starting to tremble as he walked over towards her.

'A woman of the book,' said Macleod. 'You really must have believed if you went out as a missionary. You must know him, but you haven't said anything about being happy.'

'It's not our job to be happy. It's what the Lord gives, Inspector. You should know that.'

'What did He give you?' asked Macleod. 'What did He give you, more than you can handle?'

'We were fighting with the heathens out there, ungodly, godless, no idea who He was. Then you had Georgie coming along with her crosses and these evangelicals, whipping them up, not showing due reverence in front of God. It was hard times, hard times to make a difference.'

'I'm sure it was,' said Macleod. 'What difference did you make?'

'I brought them God.'

'And what happened?' asked Macleod. 'Why did you all leave?'

'God gave what he gave,' said Angusina. 'He gave with one hand and he took it with the other.'

Even Macleod was getting tired of this religious speak and he turned away back to Daniel. 'You all just left of your own accord?'

'Reassigned,' said Daniel, but Macleod could see the trembling lip.

'They were all brought here. Why did you bring them all here, Miss Smart?'

'I didn't know they knew each other. Father didn't know they knew each other. None of us did.'

'Why would you?'

'I told you we didn't handle that. They were picked out, the people from here, picked out by others. Father just built the place and left me to run it. There's nothing more to it than that, Inspector.'

'He said it was his idea, the build, all of it.'

'Not quite, Inspector, not quite. There was someone else. Father had someone running Smart Construction for him and the man had ties to the island.'

'Ties?' asked Macleod.

'Yes. He had a woman here. Although he couldn't say who she was.'

'That's the trouble with it,' said Angusina. 'People, they don't uphold God's ways and then this happens.'

'Yet you won't speak to me of what happened. You'll sit there lying, pretending nothing happened. Just because you don't voice the words, it doesn't mean you're not lying,' said Macleod. Angusina turned away from him. He turned back to Janey Smart. 'What was the person's name?'

'It was a project manager, Sandy, Alexander Cheshire, although, he spoke for my father when it came to business. You see, father liked to keep a low profile behind things so Alexander operated like he was father. Everywhere he went, he got the name of Mr. Smart. He even went to offices because of what father ran behind it all. You have to understand that my father was quite shady in his dealings. He wouldn't stoop to murder, though.'

Macleod scratched his head. 'Hang on a minute, so you're telling me that your father didn't sign the books, he didn't keep the money? He had someone else appear there for him?'

'He had to,' said Janey. 'He'd been caught out previously with business, so invented a whole new character. Then that character had to turn up. Well, his face was known. Mr. Smart became somebody, a face everyone knew.'

'So,' said Macleod. 'When I've been told that your father's gone to Canada, when we went to check his house, he hasn't. Has he?'

'No, father hasn't gone. He's gone elsewhere, and no, he hasn't told me where.'

'So, the person allegedly in Canada, is Alexander Cheshire, am I correct?'

'Yes.'

'Do you know if Alexander Cheshire did go to Canada?'

'No idea,' said Janey. 'Once he left here, he certainly didn't come back and he never said who his partner was on the island.'

'Was he planning on staying here, though?' asked Macleod.

'He talked of it, and he seemed keen on it,' said Janey.

'Well, he's not here, certainly he's not around,' Macleod mused. 'Your father's gone off into hiding. Are you sure you're not connected in this, Miss Smart? Sounds to me that you've got your hands all over it, you and your father.'

Hope walked up behind Macleod, whispered in his ear, 'Maybe she was or maybe the person on the island, the one Alexander Cheshire was with, had their fingers in the pie too.'

Macleod turned around and looked at Daniel. 'I want to know what happened in Delta camp.'

'Nothing happened, Inspector. I keep telling you that.'

'You keep lying to me time and time again, but we'll find out. Everyone, stay here,' said Macleod. 'McGrath, with me.' Macleod walked outside of the room into the hallway and Hope followed him.

'They're stalling, I'm not getting anywhere. I'm not breaking through. Maybe your touch is needed.'

'What do you mean, my touch?'

'I'm the hard-nosed crusty old policeman. You're fresh-faced, bright, someone we might talk to. Make yourself available.'

'I don't follow what you mean.'

'Hope, I'm not being funny. Daniel, stay close. You'll make a better connection, as a woman and you're much younger than him. Don't get me wrong, it's not like he's going to hit on you or anything, but I can see that connection when he looks at you, when he talks to you. Be close because that guy is ready to break and when he does, I need the full detail from him. He'll give it to you, not to me.'

'In the meantime,' said Hope, 'what? We just keep them here, sweat them out?'

'Keep them together, keep them where we can all see them. I have a feeling another one will try, another one will go and jump, if we don't keep an eye on them. There's something tying them together, some emotional trauma that's causing this. I don't know how it works yet, Hope, but it does, and somebody brought them here to relive it, that much is clear.'

'So, we just sit with them, doing nothing else?'

'We don't do anything else. There's not a lot else we can do here except continue to hassle and keep the pressure on. Don't worry, we will be doing something else.' He reached out for his phone.

'Yes, Clarissa.'

'Ross filled me in on the detail. Good work, Sergeant. I got another job for you.'

'Okay,' said Clarissa, 'what?'

'You visited the banker to find out about Mr. Smart. Mr. Smart is not Mr. Smart. It was a person moonlighting as Mr. Smart, Alexander Cheshire. That was his actual name. Mr. Smart has not been seen but runs things from the background. I need you to get into Alexander Cheshire and then find the real Mr. Smart.

'You don't want us to find Alexander Cheshire? It might be easier. If we can get him, he might tell us where the other guy is,' said Clarissa.

'I don't think Alexander Chester's alive. That's my guess. The problem is I don't know who killed him. You might have to go into your contacts. You might have to go into places where the money talks. Find them for me, Clarissa and find them fast.'

'Yes, boss.' The phone went dead. Macleod put his phone

in his pocket. He looked back into the common room where Hope had entered and was floating around Daniel. It was that time again. The pieces were in motion and he had to wait for them to deliver. He hated times like this.

Chapter 18

It was late in the evening as Clarissa carried a cup of coffee and placed it in front of DC Ross.

'Ross, are we there yet?'

Ross looked up, struggling to force a smile before putting his head back down and looking at the notes on his deck.

'It's not me. It's the boss. He said he wanted them quick.'

'I don't mean to be disrespectful, Sarge, but can you just go away somewhere? I may have this. I need to think it through.'

'Well, there's no need to be like that.' As she turned and began to walk out of the office, deciding to go down to the canteen to get something to eat, she made her way down the steps. At eight o'clock at night, the canteen was quiet. The evening shift would be changing over in a couple of hours, which meant that they mainly were out on the town doing their beat or up in their offices. Despite this, she was able to pick up a chicken curry and sat with a plate, spooning the mouthfuls in but not really enjoying it.

She found this bit hard, having to wait on Ross, having to wait on detail. She was out of her depth with records, but records were all they had. Ross had been investigating every scrap of paper, every bill that Smart Construction had and pulling together possible links to the man behind it. There were a number of rather dubious payments and he was trying to trace back the bank accounts they had come from. Many of them were held in strange names, people he could not locate, and he was searching back through those accounts to see what money had come through as well. All she needed was a tie-in name, someone she could go to and put pressure on.

The doors of the canteen flew open and Ross came running over to the table, throwing a piece of paper down on it.

'We need to go.'

'We need to go? Why?' asked Clarissa. 'You found something?'

'You bet I found something. That man, there.' Clarissa looked down and saw a name written on the paper.

'Dominic Lobo? What sort of a name's that?' asked Clarissa.

'Dom Lobo, not Dominic. Dom Lobo, the comedian.'

'The comedian?'

'You're not with me, are you?' said Ross.

'No,' said Clarissa. 'Never heard of him.'

'Dom Lobo, kind of a modern comic. Maybe you wouldn't get him. He was involved in a series of dubious dealings with some new houses constructed on the edge of Inverness. Nothing proved, but I have got several payments tracing through.'

'Enough to link him in properly with it, to show misdoing?'

'No,' said Ross. 'We're not lifting him on anything, but so far nobody knows he's involved. He's also an up and coming comic. I mean, he's starting to rise up in the circuit. He's doing a gig tonight down in town. Quite a significant one. He's on stage at 9:00 p.m.'

'And what? We need to go and haul him in instead?'

'I was thinking you could go and have a word,' said Ross.

'With what?' asked Clarissa. 'You said you've linked some payments in but there's no proof. There's nothing I can actually say to him. Is there?'

'No, but the houses on the Fortnaught Estate, he used money from other places, dirty money, for his share. We can't prove it, but I can get this information to a paper.'

Clarissa smiled. 'I thought you were really strict when I first joined, Als. Solid copper, wouldn't do anything on the dirty side. But you know what, I'm beginning to like you even more. Sit down for two minutes. Give me more of the detail.'

'And I was thinking if you could do it just before he goes on, so he's in a rush.'

Clarissa laughed. 'That's too good. That is like something I would do.'

Ten minutes later, the pair were in the small sports car racing through Inverness. Clarissa parked up on a side street before they walked round to the small venue downtown, a comedy store that had been open for only six months. As they entered through the front, Ross showed his warrant card and asked to be taken through to the back to Dominic Lobo. The person at the front door called for the manager, and when he arrived, Clarissa stepped forward, engaging the man in conversation.

'We're just here to speak to Dominic Lobo. Police business.'

'It's not going to be long, is it?' asked the man. 'He's due on stage in ten minutes.'

'It will be as long as it takes, frankly. Oh, I don't know. How long can your guests wait?'

'They can't wait. They've paid for this. We upped the ticket price for this one. It's a full house.'

'A full house? Oh dear. Have you got plenty of drink in?'

'Why?' asked the man.

'Because you're going to need to keep them happy while we're doing our interview.'

'Can't you wait until after?'

'What?' said Clarissa. 'Wait while he tells jokes up there? Wait for a possible thief? Guy's a criminal. To go in and have a laugh and earn some money? Not worth my badge. My Inspector will be all over me for that. No, you need to take me there now.'

The house manager turned and marched through the back corridors of the building down to a small door with a rather bizarre star stuck on it. He knocked on it, heard a 'Come in,' and entered, Clarissa and Ross in tow.

'This is Dom Lobo,' said the house manager. 'Dom, these are police officers. They want to speak to you. You're on in ten minutes. If you're not out in five, I'm going to find someone else.'

'Hey,' said Dom. 'What do you mean? This is it. This is the big gig.'

'Then you'd better be quick with us,' said Clarissa. 'Because I think this man here is going to get someone else.'

The house manager stood impatiently, looking at Dominic, who Clarissa could see was already in a flap. After thirty seconds, Ross walked over and tapped the house manager on the shoulder.

'We generally like to interview people on their own,' he said.

'Four and a half minutes, Dom. You better be out that door.'

Once the door closed, Dominic looked over. He was a balding man, barely five feet six, but he was also really jumpy. 'You're getting a little bit impatient there, aren't you?' said

158

Clarissa. 'You've got four minutes left.'

'What's this about?' he said. 'Do you realise what you're doing? This is the chance of a lifetime for me. There's people out there watching this, people out there who'll take me up to the big time.'

'People out there who would not be impressed to hear about the Fortnaught Estate,' said Clarissa.

'What do you mean, Fortnaught Estate?'

'The money, the money for that partnership. You threw money in, didn't you, Dominic? You threw money at it, but where did that money come from and who did you get it from? Trouble is, Dominic, that we found links to that money. We don't think it was all kosher.'

'Says who? You don't know anything about that money. I got that from my accounts.'

'Yes, I saw it there,' said Ross. 'I saw it in your accounts. I've also seen where it came from, the accounts that fed into it, the people who own those accounts, people who don't take kindly to publicity.'

'No, no, there's nothing you can prove, I'm sure about that. The accountant said all of that was untraceable.'

'The word untraceable's bandied about a lot,' said Ross.

'Indeed,' said Clarissa. 'Untraceable doesn't mean that there can't be a link made from it. Something to say, "Hang on a minute, that looks like it could come from here."'

'But there's no proof,' said Dominic. 'There's no proof on any of that. You're just farting in the wind here. You're just dangling stuff in front of me, hoping that I'll squeal.'

'If I had the full evidence, I would arrest you. I'd pull you in before this gig had even started,' said Clarissa. 'DC Ross here will do everything by the book; he's good like that. He can follow detail, he can pin everything down, but he said to me, "I can't pin everything down on him. I don't have enough to prosecute," so I said, "What do you have, Ross?" Do you know what he said to me; he said, "Well, I've probably got enough for the papers."'

Dom's face froze. 'What do you mean, the papers?'

'Enough for a story,' said Clarissa. 'Enough that your name will be branded with that estate, with all the difficulties that came out of it, where the funding came from. I reckon they could run the story for nearly six months.'

'What do you want?' asked Dom. 'Why are you waving that in front of me?'

'Smart Construction,' said Clarissa. 'I want the owner of Smart Construction.'

'Went to Canada,' said Dom. 'Haven't heard from him since. Bit of a shock for us all, him going to Canada.'

'He did,' said Ross. 'However, you still make payments to him since he went to Canada. Payments that have been acted on, keeping it in cash in this country.'

'I don't know where he is.'

'We know about the man at the front of it. Alexander Cheshire.' Dom's face froze. 'We know he was the front, the smiling face because the man behind Smart Construction couldn't own a business because of his dealings from before. I need to know who he is, I need to know where to find him because he's got information on a case that we're working on.'

'He doesn't like to be found,' said Dom. There was a rap on the door.

'Dom, I swear, thirty seconds; if you're not out here, you're cancelled.'

'Thirty seconds,' said Clarissa. 'Oh, twenty-seven.'

'More like twenty-five,' said Ross. Clarissa flashed a smile at him before turning to Dom. 'Name, address, and I'm not coming back for you at all. I don't really give a damn about what you did up there on that estate, but I'll wave it in every paper if you don't give me that name.'

'That's a form of extortion,' said the man.

'I'm not sure that's technically correct,' said Ross.

'No, but he is right, it's certainly some form of coercion. However, fifteen seconds.'

'Oh, more like ten,' said Ross.

'Okay,' said Dom, and Clarissa could see the sweat running down his forehead. 'Kieran, Kieran Jones. Aviemore, quite a smart lodge up the back. 32, just beyond a petrol station.'

The door flung open and the house manager marched in.

'It's okay,' said Clarissa, smiling. 'Mr. Lobo is about to go on and give the performance of his life, and hopefully we won't be speaking to him again afterwards, if everything's in order.' Clarissa watched the man shake as he walked out of the door and the house manager turned to them.

'I assume you can see yourselves out, I've got a show to run.'

'Thank you for your assistance, sir; it's much appreciated.'

'Ma'am.'

'Let's get going, Als. Looks like it's a drive to Aviemore.'

'Can you get the top up on the car then?' said Ross. 'It was blooming freezing getting here.'

* * *

There was a wind howling around Aviemore, but it was dry. Ross had his collar up when the car pulled in at the lodge beyond the petrol station. 'Dom said number 32 on the door,' noted Clarissa as she hopped out of her car and strode over towards the front door.

'What, you're just going to bang it? What if he runs?'

'He won't run,' said Clarissa. 'Not someone like this. Just trust me, I've dealt with people like this before.' Ross followed her to the front door and watched as she thundered on it with her fist. The door opened, and an older man smiled. 'Clarissa Urquhart,' he said. 'Wow, been a while.'

'Kieran, what have you been up to? Naughty boy by the sounds of it. I need to have a chat with you.'

'Who's your playboy?' said the man, grinning and showing yellow teeth.

'This is DC Ross, here about a case. I don't think you're involved, but I need to be sure.'

'Come in,' he said. 'There's a fire on.' Clarissa stepped inside, and Kieran turned to her. 'Is he okay?'

'Als is grand. It's okay; it's all off the record. He knows that, don't you, Alan?' Ross felt uncomfortable but nodded. 'Mr. Jones and I have met before, you see,' said Clarissa, 'regarding a certain artefact which he had purchased that was a fake. I was involved in the case finding where the real one was and we did a bit of work together.'

'Your colleague's quite something, DC Ross.'

'You have to understand, Alan, that Kieran is quite the businessman. He's forceful, he's brutal, but he's not illegal, never illegal.'

'Well. Only in the sense that I have a bit of a front because I was gazumped back in the day. Not allowed to run a business anymore. All has to be done with somebody else's name.'

'Just details,' said Clarissa. 'Now, have you got any whisky?'

'Of course. Of course,' said Kieran. 'Please, sit down.'

162

The man went across to a cupboard, opened it, took out three tumblers and began to pour whisky. 'Just the two,' said Clarissa.

'What?' said the man. 'You turned over a new leaf?'

'No, but DC Ross is driving back. It's my car and we are the police, so there's no way we're getting nicked for drunk driving. Good lad, Als,' said Clarissa, at which the man laughed.

'She was always like this. Play anybody, though we do let her.'

'He has to. I'm his boss.'

'Senior colleague,' said Ross and Clarissa laughed.

'Touché.'

Taking the drink, Clarissa knocked about half of it back before walking over towards the large fire in the living room. 'Alexander Cheshire,' said Clarissa. 'He was fronting Smart Construction for you.'

'Yes, and he was doing a darn good job of it,' said Kieran. 'And then he upped and vanished. Allegedly went to Canada.'

'Allegedly?' queried Ross.

'Yes, allegedly. Not been heard from since. I'm trying to work out what happened, but it's not easy. Especially with the deaths over on Eigg. Trying to keep a bit of a distance.'

'Time to tell me what it's about,' said Clarissa. 'We've got residents over there jumping off into the sea. My boss is there believing that murder's afoot. How did you get into it all?'

Kieran downed the whisky, put the tumbler back down and poured himself another. He looked over to Clarissa, who downed hers, put her tumbler down beside his. As he poured another two, he stood beside the fire with her.

'The thing is, I was at a refugee do, Refugees of War, down in Glasgow. An event where a Margaret McCormick was taking part. Apparently, she'd been out in Africa, had seen a lot of this refugee thing. I didn't know; I was just doing it for business. Put a bit of money behind this and whatever, you know, keep the reputation up. Able to cover some of the dodgier aspects of business.'

Ross could see Clarissa's smile and nod. He was distinctly uncomfortable with the fact that this man was talking about how to cover up breaking the law. Clarissa was completely engaging with him, her eyes fixed on his.

'Well, this Mrs. McCormick, she talked about Eigg, how beautiful it was, the singing sands, et cetera, and she says to me it'd make a great retirement home, and she knew the line of business I was in. So, we got talking afterwards. She showed me photographs and it went from there. I mean, it's a great site, wonderful idea, but after the initial build idea, that was me stepping back. Alexander then stepped in in front. He did everything after the initial design. I gave my thoughts, then left Alexander to get it all up and running.'

'So, you didn't get involved with who the residents were?'

'No,' said Kieran. 'Hell, no. Why would I want to get involved in that? People sitting there talking this and talking that. No, I let Alexander work that out with her.'

'And that's why you're stepping out of it, isn't it?' said Clarissa. 'You know something's afoot.'

'You're darn right something's afoot,' said Kieran. 'Some-body's able to kill at will. I'm not going to make my connection known in there until I know who it is. Don't get me wrong. I want to know what's happened to Alexander. Caused me no end of hassle having to get a new front person up, and with Janey tied into it.'

'So, Janey is your daughter?' said Clarissa.

164

'Oh, yeah. You remember the little girl?'

'She was a baby,' said Clarissa.

'Yep, but that was her. Janey doesn't see eye to eye with me with what I do. But do you know what? I have got her off this stupid idea of being a tennis star. She might do all right out there.'

'Was she involved with making the decisions about who came in?' asked Ross.

'I don't know, but she's out there with them. I am worried for her,' said Kieran, staring at Clarissa. 'I really am.'

'Tell me about Margaret McCormick,' said Clarissa.

'She was a passionate woman. Very big about the refugees. You get people at these things that speak, and yeah, it's just a dinner do. Oh, she spoke from the heart. Got her degree in psychology. It was funny because her father was at the place as well. But not her mother, just her father. He was doing like a hypnotism act. I had to laugh. Didn't work on me, but it worked on quite a few people. You know, the usual thing, the rooms flooding, get yourself out of here. Some bloke sitting on a woman's knee pretending it was his mum. Some girl running around professing undying love to somebody four times her age. It was very good, but she was the star performer. So passionate about what she was doing. Real sense of injustice.'

'Where is she now?' asked Clarissa.

'I don't know. I mean there were basic addresses for her, but everywhere I've contacted, she's not there. Alexander had other contacts for her, but they've gone with him. Turns out she was rather secretive.'

'Anything else you can tell us?' asked Clarissa.

'No, I don't know anything else. I really don't.'

Clarissa downed the tumbler, placed it down, and turned

to Ross. 'Chauffeur, get in the car.' Ross let the comment go and walked toward the door, catching the keys Clarissa threw to him. As he sat in the car waiting, he saw Clarissa at the doorstep where Kieran Jones embraced her. He then gave her a peck on the cheek and made his way over, escorting her to the car. When she was inside, he returned to his front door and waved as she drove off.

'You okay?' asked Ross as he saw a tear in Clarissa's eyes.

'Fine, Als. Fine.'

'You two seemed kind of close,' said Ross.

'Are you okay with that?' said Clarissa. 'It's probably best if you don't mention that bit to Macleod.'

'Okay, but that man's daughter is out in the middle of all our investigations.'

'True. Probably fearing for her. He really is. He has told us the truth in there. He wants to get to the bottom of this as well. He's a bit of a cad, a bit of a wild man, plays the rules loose, but he's no murderer. He's quite something.'

'You certainly seem very taken with him,' said Ross.

'I saved his life once and he was very grateful. We nearly—well, we nearly had something.'

'Do you want to tell me any more about it?' said Ross. 'Your job was in the art world. This seems very intriguing.'

'No, I don't. Drive on, chauffeur. We need to talk to the boss.'

Chapter 19

Hope was standing looking at Daniel, the Englishman, who was sitting on a settee, his head in his hands. She made her way up beside him, sat down, and watched as he raised his head, looking at her.

'Is there something I can do for you?' he asked. There were tears in his eyes, and his shoulders were slumped.

'I was wondering if there was anything I could do for you,' asked Hope. 'You seem burdened.'

'Well, that's because I am. Your Inspector was right about the Congo, but we thought that was all behind us. We thought that time was gone. It's only ever Angusina who said that your sins come back to pay. You can't keep the past away. I guess that's true.'

'What are you talking about?' asked Hope.

'The time out there, Hope, was not a good one. At first, it was. I was young, I had a new job, but the change to the place was hard. Those days you didn't have mobile phones, you didn't have satellite. You couldn't just connect with anyone else. You were out there on your own making decisions with the civil disturbance going around you. It was scary. I was in my twenties and I'd never seen such ferocity. It sounds racist now, but they were all black people as well. I had no experience of them. Yes, we had black people in the country, but not like this, speaking languages I didn't understand. Most of the black people I had seen were refined. They were like us, like the English almost. Yet, even here, of course we had trouble. But out there they were wearing different things. Nowadays, you look at it and you say it's just their attire, it's their garb, what they wear, it's just tribal, there's nothing to it, but back then it was threatening. There was such squalor with it as well. I found that hard to take. I just wanted away from it.'

'But what happened, Daniel? Lots of people have gone to Africa with awkward situations, difficult times, but they don't end up running into the sea. You can tell me, it's okay.' She placed her hand on Daniel's.

'We were in the Delta Camp, refugee camp set up for them. The local tribes, they were very antagonistic towards each other. We had taken people in from a tribe that the locals said had attacked them. It was ten years ago or something. I never quite followed the language but there was bitterness. They saw us helping them. We said we would help anyone, in fact we had a sister tribe in Beta Camp but that was some distance off and reports weren't coming through clearly. It didn't fit the agenda of what certain people wanted, either. It's funny—in some ways, they're so like us.'

'But what actually happened, Daniel?'

'We got word one night they were coming to attack. We could tell because the tribe were scared. We had gathered the children together, all the youngsters; we were going to lead them away when we got cornered.'

'When you say we, who do you mean?'

'All the white people. The tribe coming, they were scared in some ways about us, because they were coming to kill these children but with us there, they stopped. They stopped and asked us to hand them over, said we could go but if we didn't hand them over, they would just kill us as well. Sergeant, they had machetes ready to use them. I was twenty, I'd never seen the like of it. I had been brought up in a home that never saw violence. I was refined, educated. I didn't know anything of the world like this. I had Georgie, a nun, with me. Angusina. Missionaries from America. I had nobody capable of standing up for the fight. We would be massacred.'

'What did you do?' asked Hope. Daniel bent over and began to cry. He then sat up, suddenly looked at Hope, his eyes wide, white with tears streaming down his face.

'We gave them the kids. We left those little ones and went. God, Sergeant, we heard them, heard them when we left. They didn't wait. They didn't let us go and then take these kids somewhere else. They butchered them there. We never saw it happen, but we heard everything.'

Hope felt her own hands shaking as the man spoke, tears coming to her own eyes. 'We left them,' said Daniel. 'We should have protected them.'

'Then what?' said Hope.

'We managed to make our way to a different camp. After a couple of days' walk we were found. The Major your Inspector spoke of, he found us and he asked us what happened and we said to him there was an attack and we escaped. I didn't tell him about the kids. But he was going to the camp, so I guess he would have found out.'

'Did you all get out?' asked Hope.

'No. There was a number of white people that died in the

169

initial attack. Three of them, I think. So long ago I can't remember them. And then we went off and lived our lives. I mean we did okay. We coped. Georgina gave up being a nun. I guess she just couldn't live with it. Angusina is as morbid as the day she ever was, but the rest of us, we did.'

'And my aunt was with you.'

Daniel looked at Hope. 'Don't judge her. You weren't there. She was young. She couldn't cope with it. She would have been dead. What would you have done?'

'I might have fought for them,' said Hope.

'Maybe you would,' said Daniel, 'but you'd have died. I was young. I didn't want to die. They would have killed the children anyway. That's what I've been telling myself all along. It's what I've always told myself, but there were none of us there after that. We'd all gone our separate ways. I hadn't seen any of them, not been in contact. Years, then I got this letter inviting me to this retirement home. I'd done well, I had money, I could make it work. It seemed like a good place. It all seemed very soothing. Do you feel that about the place, Hope?'

Hope wondered how her boss would feel about that, having lost his own wife into the sea as a suicide. She wasn't so sure he'd find it reassuring or soothing.

'Did you not find it a surprise when you all got here? All of you suddenly reunited.'

'Of course, it was a surprise,' said Daniel, 'but what could we do? We decided to stick together to find out who was behind us. It had to have something to do with this place.'

'But then what about when Joel went? When he died?'

'We thought it was just that he had too much of it. We've all been suffering since we got together. It's all been coming back. We all hear the voices. It's like a mass hysteria. Maybe it's just

170

comeuppance. Angusina said it's the Lord paying us back.'

'I don't think the Lord works like that,' said Hope.

'Are you religious?' asked Daniel, almost an earnestness in his eyes.

'No,' said Hope, 'not in the slightest, but my boss is, and he doesn't believe God works like that either.'

'Don't feel bad about your aunt Mary. When we were here, she said to me, "I'll invite Hope down, see if she can work out what's going on." She was so proud of you. Being a detective, the work you'd done. Whenever you made the papers she'd say, "That's my Hope. That's Hope. She works with Macleod." She'd say you were the brilliance behind it, not Macleod. She'd tell us sometimes how you wrote to her saying about your Inspector being so in the old ways, a man of Lewis. Well, our woman of Harris here, Angusina, she berated Mary for your attitude, and I think that's why we stayed. There was something of those old days. In the Congo, we got on well together. You have to understand that, Hope. It just ended so bloody awfully.'

'But who's doing it?' said Hope. 'Who's killing you off?'

'Who says we're being killed off?'

'My aunt's severed arm says you're being killed off.'

Daniel ignored Hope's comment. 'Georgie, was it who said it? Georgie went along there and jumped in. You say what you like about Georgie, she was a woman of her convictions. She spoke when she saw it. She couldn't take any more and I'm not sure I can, Hope. Do you not hear them when you go down there? Well, of course, you don't because you weren't there. Your aunt heard them too. Children are coming back for us. They're paying us vengeance.'

'The children are dead,' said Hope. 'They don't come back.

There are no ghosts coming from Africa. This is something else. I will get to the bottom of this, for someone killed my aunt.' Hope stood up, fighting hard to keep the tears from falling from her eyes, and she walked off to the far corner of the room. With her head buried, she closed her eyes and tried not to see the children before her, children she'd never known. After a moment, somebody touched her shoulder.

'Are you okay?' said her boss.

'No. Seoras, it's horrible what they did, what my aunt did.'

'What do you mean?' asked Macleod.

'They were attacked. Delta Camp was attacked like they said, but they'd had the children and they kept the children safe until they got cornered by the other tribe, and the other tribe offered to let them walk if they handed the kids back over.'

'And they did, didn't they?' said Macleod.

'Yes. My aunt Mary handed over children to their death. My aunt Mary who I thought was like me. I wouldn't do it. I wouldn't have done that. I'd have fought for them. I'd have gone down tooth and nail.'

Hope felt her hand being taken by Macleod's. 'And you'd have died. You'd have died defending what you believed. You'd have died defending poor children, but you'd have died. They were in a strange land at that time, scared, and were so young. She wouldn't have been even your age by now.'

'That's no excuse,' said Hope.

'I wasn't making excuses,' said Macleod, 'and I wasn't placing blame, which you're doing. You have no idea what they were going through. The terror coursing through your aunt's veins.'

'But they are to blame. They didn't do the decent thing. They didn't defend those kids.'

'No,' said Macleod, 'but somebody else thinks the same thing. Somebody else who's out to kill. You can't blame, Hope. You can't be the judge. Every time we're the judge, we often end up being the executioner, and I won't let you do that. You're too good a person.'

Hope took a look at him and could see the pain in Seoras' eyes, a face that was looking to reach to her, begging her to stop this path she was on. 'I'm struggling to forgive her, Seoras.'

'You have to,' said Macleod, 'because if you don't, who else will? I doubt she ever forgave herself.'

Chapter 20

Macleod held Hope for the next couple of minutes while she cried on his shoulder. When she stopped and straightened up, he asked if she was okay before telling her to go to the bathroom and clean herself up. She returned, hair tied up in a ponytail behind her. Her face gave a smile while her eyes still showed red from where she'd been crying.

'Are you okay?' said Macleod. 'I will take this from here if you want. You're close to this, probably too close. I'm happy to take it myself.'

'You've got no backup here, Seoras. You need me with you.'

'That, I do,' said Seoras, 'but it doesn't matter. If this is too painful, if this is too much for you, I'd rather see you not do it.'

'No,' said Hope. 'I need to do it.'

'Okay,' said Macleod, 'but if at any time it's too much, if at any time your professional judgment is compromised, then you step out. Do you understand me? You step out and I'll get you through it.'

Hope reached forward taking Macleod's head in her hands and then kissed him on the forehead.

'She picked a good one in you, Seoras. Jane picked a good one.'

'Jane's got enough problems. She knows me too well, better than you, so come on. We need to go and talk to Janey Smart.'

'Just a moment, Seoras,' said Hope, and she hugged him tight. 'Daniel said you were the moody, grumpy inspector. You're never like that when you're a friend.' Hope stepped back and Macleod struggled to know quite what to say.

'Well then,' he said. 'Janey Smart.'

'Yes, boss,' said Hope, and marched off to the far side of the room. Macleod watched her stand and explain to the woman that the Inspector wanted to speak to her, and Hope then pointed out to the offices. Macleod followed the two women as they wound up in Janey's own office, where she took a seat behind her desk.

'What's up, Inspector? Why am I out here?'

'The residents were all together in the Congo in 1960.'

'That's correct. You've already told us that,' said Janey. 'Nothing new in that.'

'No,' said Hope, 'but they were part of a massacre. The Delta Camp they were in, was massacred.'

'Okay,' said Janey, 'so they've all suffered together.'

'Then they end up here,' said Macleod. 'The thing about the massacre was they had a large number of children in their protection, and they gave them up to those who were doing the massacre, so that they could escape.'

'That's wicked,' said Janey.

'It's survival, and I'm not here to judge them,' said Macleod. 'What I am here to do is work out who put them back together. You told me you and your father had nothing to do with it. I'm beginning to disagree. At the moment, I have officers looking for your father.'

'Alexander went to Canada, he might have known but I haven't heard from him,' said Janey.

'I don't believe that for a minute,' said Macleod. 'The man who came here initially doing the designs, Alexander stayed and built the place. He was the one who was deeply involved.'

Janey gave a fixed stare. Macleod could tell she was weighing up the options of what to say.

'Don't bother, Janey,' said Hope. 'He's cleverer than that.'

'I don't understand the business. Father said that Alexander would be here, and I would have to pretend he was my father, but we never did much. We went for meals together, whatever, enough for the charade.'

'Do you know his real name?' said Macleod. The woman shook her head. 'Of course not. Your father's too clever for that. What's your father's real name? What's your real name, Janey?'

'You tell me, Inspector. I won't give him up like that. He's not a bad man, but he's mixes in circles that you keep your head down in. This whole thing about the business, he's not allowed to own one due to past errors, so it has to be in somebody else's name and the fictional Mr. Smart was a good person to have. If I didn't ask who the man really was who was here pretending to be my father, then I couldn't betray him, so I didn't.'

'What's your real name, Janey?'

'I am Janey Smart. It's on my birth certificate.'

'Why?' said Hope. 'Even at that age?'

'My birth certificate has no father on it. It has only a mother. Alison Smart died when I was seven. Up to that point, I barely knew my father. He kept her in a style with food and lodgings, and my mother never had to work, devoting all her time to me, but I never saw my father. My mother occasionally worked at a club and he came in one night and they hit it off. My mother said he never forced himself upon her. It was mutual. They were so excited that they forgot to take precautions. Nine months later, I turned up. He stood by her, did right by her, but he had family at the time. His other wife is now dead. I have a stepbrother and a stepsister, but they don't know me.'

'It's all pretty convoluted,' said Hope. 'How did you manage to have a life like that?'

'I went off to tennis school. As I said before, I was pretty good, but I never made the grade and now he's sent me up here. The one thing you can say about my father is he will look after his own. You may not like him as a business person as he's maybe a little bit dodgy, but he looks after his kin.'

'Where is he?' asked Macleod.

'I have not been in touch in over three months. He's doing that for a reason. He's never stayed that quiet for that long. He doesn't give me addresses. He tells me where to meet. He wants to make sure that I don't know anything that can give him up, not because of people like you, Inspector, but because of the nastier people. In fact, most people don't even know I'm his daughter.'

'What is your father's real name?' asked Macleod.

Janey laughed. 'I'd tell you if I could. I don't know his surname. I did once find out he's called Kieran.'

Macleod shook his head. 'You were involved with who was selected here, weren't you?'

'To a point,' said Janey, 'but like I said, we had the locals here doing it.'

'What about your father or your pretend father, rather? Was he involved?'

'Quite heavily.'

'You see, I have a problem, Janey. I have a problem that you seem to be in a position of trust with these people. You live close by. You're around the grounds. You organised the people to be here. However you've done it, I think you've pulled them together.'

'Why?' said Janey. 'Why? Why would I start killing these people off?'

'Because you have a common experience and it's worked out well for you. The trauma they all suffered before, it's driving them into a mass hysteria, and you can slowly bump them off, and then you'll get new people in. You said to me your father, he doesn't bother with you at this place. This is yours now. I think he deliberately brought in people who are mentally damaged in an attempt to end their life quickly to make more money.'

Hope started and looked over at the Inspector.

'That's preposterous,' said Janey. 'I have nothing to do with this. You do realise that this is screwing me over. You do realise that this is going wrong for me. I said to you before, "Who on earth is going to turn around and actually live in a place like this, where everybody keeps dying?" You can't just bump people off at a rate that quick. Georgie—Georgie jumped. I wasn't there. You saw her die. It wasn't me.'

'Regardless,' said Macleod, 'somebody killed Mary. Somebody cut her arm off. I think I have enough to charge you. I think I have enough certainly to hold you under suspicion of murder.'

'Is that what you want, Inspector?' asked Hope. Macleod could see she was unsure, but Hope was refraining from saying it outright, telling him she thought he was wrong. This was as much a point as she could make in front of a suspect.

'We shall hold Janey Smart under the suspicion of murder while we investigate further. You'll not be with any of the residents at this time, Miss Smart; instead, you'll place yourself under a house arrest. I'll dig further, but I can't wait for the weather. Do you understand me, Ms. Smart?'

Janey Smart nodded. 'How do you know it's me? You haven't got any evidence.'

Macleod looked around the room. 'Search the office, Hope.' Janey sat on her desk with Macleod beside her while Hope started to open every drawer. 'Don't forget the locked one,' said Macleod, and Hope continued taking keys from Janey, opening all of her desk drawers and searching through.

'There's nothing,' said Hope.

'Far corner, that bottom drawer of the filing cabinet.'

'There's nothing in there. It's waste. It's all rusted.'

'Nonetheless,' said Macleod, 'search it.' Hope went over to the filing cabinet that'd seen better days, and as she started opening the drawers, Macleod heard the clink of metal. Everything could do with a little bit of lubrication, and he winced at the pain his ears felt as the bottom drawer was opened. Hope looked inside, and putting on a glove from her pocket, she reached inside the drawer and held something up.

'What's that?' asked Macleod.

'It's a golf club head, Inspector,' said Hope. 'Joel Grimshaw was missing one of his set of clubs. If you look at it, it's signed, signed by the Ryder Cup team numerous years ago.'

'Why have you got that?' asked Macleod.

'I didn't,' said Janey. 'I've never seen that before. That drawer is open. Anyone could put that there.'

'I think I've heard enough,' said Macleod. 'Sergeant, arrest Janey Smart on suspicion of murder.' Macleod watched Hope go behind the woman and place handcuffs on her. She then read her rights and went to take her out of the office.

'Where do I take her, Inspector?' asked Hope.

'Place her in the spare room, the guest room of the building. We'll remain on guard until the storm outside passes.' Macleod watched Hope escort Janey Smart through the common room into the spare set of bedrooms for guests at the facility. Having installed Janey in one of the rooms, Hope locked it and then stood outside as Macleod joined her.

'That's set them talking,' said Hope.

'It has indeed,' said Macleod, 'but I needed her locked up.'

'Why? How's that golf head got there? Who in the right mind would hide it in that place? I mean, I've heard about putting things in plain sight, but that's ridiculous. Too easy to find.'

'Exactly,' said Macleod. 'too simple, Hope. Somebody is trying to place the blame elsewhere. Somebody has realised that we believe it's murder and now they're trying to give us a culprit.'

'Who, sir?' asked Hope.

'I don't know, and I'm not sure the answer's here, but at least in the meantime, Janey Smart is safe.'

'How do you mean?' asked Hope.

'A man who went to Canada, who I think isn't around anymore, having been dispatched by our murderer. It will soon come out that he wasn't the real Mr. Smart, then our murderer is going to have to cover up again.'

'They'll come for Janey.'

'Exactly, so we're not leaving our manager like this. You and

I will stick here. Keep the residents in front of our eyes.'

'Okay, Seoras. You see, you did need me. You couldn't do this on your own.'

'I've always needed you, Hope,' said Macleod. 'With time, you'll realise that.'

Chapter 21

Back at the police station, Ross sat down behind his computer while Clarissa made some more coffee. It could be a long night for they had to track down Mary McCormack. There would no doubt be many of them throughout Scotland and it wouldn't be a case of just simply pulling up an address but rather trying to attach some credence to why this was the person they were looking for.

'There you go,' said Clarissa, placing a coffee in front of Ross.

'Can you make a phone call for me?' he asked. 'Through to the offices of the council?'

'The council offices won't be open,' said Clarissa.

'No,' said Ross. 'You need to get somebody up. I need access into the files. I can't do it from here.'

'Not a problem.' She picked up one of the phones on the desk and looked over for a number from Ross. After a quick search, he passed it over and Clarissa made the call.

'What's the big deal?' said the man on the other end. 'Do you know what time of night it is? We closed the offices ages ago.'

'This is Detective Sergeant Clarissa Urquhart and I need your assistance, sir, and I need it urgently.'

'Well, I suppose if that's the way you're playing it, what can I do?'

'I need you to get me access to your departmental records.'

'What for?'

'I need to see if someone's changed their name.'

'Right. Well, I can authorise that,' said the man, 'but I have no idea how to do it. Can you give me a minute? I'll ring you back. What's your number?'

It took about ten minutes before Ross was in contact with someone savvy enough with the technology who knew what they were doing. Together, the two managed to patch up a link and Ross began barrelling through the array of names in front of him. 'Did he say Margaret McCormack or Mary McCormack?'

'Kieran said Margaret.'

'But Margaret and Mary, it's sometimes interchanged up here in Scotland, isn't it?'

'Or it's a double name, Margaret Mary,' said Clarissa. 'It can be a funny one.'

'Well, I'll spread it wide. Cast the net and see what comes up.'

Twenty minutes later, Ross and Clarissa were sitting with at least fifty names in front of them. There were a number of addresses as well as other details.

'We need to get a rough age on her,' said Ross. 'Clarissa, I think anybody under twenty is too young and from what description Kieran gave us about her I don't think she's going to be in her seventies or above, so I'll rule those ages out. That bring us down to thirty-five different names. Right, we start going through the addresses, we start going through everything that's on here and just see what digs up. Are you okay to assist me with that?' said Ross.

'I'm not totally inept,' said Clarissa. 'Computers were just not always in front of us at a young age.'

Ross gave Clarissa a small section of the names and asked her to start looking there but he burrowed into the rest of them. He was aware that every ten minutes Clarissa would stand up, walk around the room before sitting down and she was clearly not happy sitting in front of a computer.

'Something wrong with your seat?' he asked.

'How do you do this?' said Clarissa. 'How do you sit here?'

'It's no wonder the boss says your reports are short.'

'My reports are fine, concise and to the point. That's all you need. No point being long-winded.'

'Anyway, have you got anything?'

'Well, there's a Mary McCormack and she changed her name. She's now Moira Gladstone and we have got some previous addresses here for her.'

'Gladstone?' said Ross. 'You sure about that?'

'Yes, it says Gladstone here.'

'Show me that record on my screen.' Clarissa stepped round, pointed out the name on Ross's large list. He clicked through various windows and saw a long list of addresses. The woman indeed had changed her name to Moira Gladstone. He then delved into her records further. 'Do you see this, here?' said Ross.

'This's her birth certificate, isn't it?'

'Yes. Moira Gladstone. Interesting, isn't it?'

'Right? Why is it interesting?'

'Look at the mother,' said Ross.

'Never mind the mother. Look at the father, Daniel. That's . . . is that Daniel what's his name? Daniel Edwards. The guy at our retirement home.'

'Well, yes, that's Daniel Edwards, but look at the mother.'

'Isla Gladstone, yes.'

'If you go back into the Congo and look at the details we have for the Congo, Isla Gladstone was there.'

'What do you mean she was there?'

'Isla Gladstone was in the Congo. She was one of the white workers.'

'But they all escaped. That's our group in the retirement home.'

'She was there. She just wasn't with them when the attack happened. She must have been off on R&R or something, but she wasn't there.'

'You might be onto something, Ross. What further detail is there about her?'

'Isla Gladstone died, took her own life apparently. Not far from here. There must be a record somewhere. Hang on.' Ross began to delve into police records, cross-referencing the name Isla Gladstone. Five minutes later he was able to produce a case file where one of the detectives had gone round, anxious to prove that the woman had indeed committed suicide.

'Can we bring those files up?' said Clarissa. She was now parked in front of her own laptop and Ross made the files appear on screen. Clarissa buried herself reading quickly.

'It says here, Ross, that she was depressed. They were worried about her for a long time.'

'Did it say why?' asked Ross.

'From her experiences in Africa. There's a guy from the home makes a comment. He's quoted as saying she was haunted. Haunted by things that had happened. He said her suicide was not unexpected, but that they couldn't prevent it.'

'And she's the mother of Moira Gladstone.'

'But there's no one named that, is there? Not over her time at home. None of the residents are Gladstone.'

'No, but there's that link. There's that link to Daniel,' said Ross. 'I wonder what caused her to die. I wonder what drove her mad, made her want to commit suicide.'

'This statement was made by one of the carers for her, people that worked with her. Can we see if we can find an address for that person?'

'William Thomas. William Thomas,' chuntered Ross. 'Hang on.' He began to type into the computer again. Clarissa stood up from her chair, stepped around the desk and looked over Ross's shoulder. He was whipping through databases again and then he suddenly pointed at the screen.

'There. Still working. That's the home for her. That's where he works now. There's a contact number. There's an out of hours emergency as well.'

'Excellent,' said Clarissa. 'Give me that phone!' She dialled in and got a rather sleepy-sounding woman on the other end.

'Yes, this is Castlemaine Retirement Home. Oh, Mr. Thomas? Yes, Mr. Thomas works for us. He'll be at home at the moment.'

'Would you have an address for him?' asked Clarissa.

'We're not into giving our addresses out.'

'This is DS Clarissa Urquhart and I'm in pursuit of a murderer. Mr. Thomas may be able to give us some valuable information. I request you give me his address now.'

Ross could hear Clarissa using the *I'm-now-serious* voice, the one she used when she wanted things to happen straightaway.

'Oh, right,' said the woman. 'Of course. Do you mind if I ring ahead and tell him you're coming?'

'Not at all,' said Clarissa. 'We're not looking for Mr. Thomas in connection with any wrongdoing. He may have some information, some background he's able to help us with.'

Ross watched Clarissa write something down on a pad and then rip off a piece of paper. 'Come on, Als. We're off, other side of Inverness.' Clarissa turned without waiting, grabbed her coat, and went out of the door. Ross noticed the scarf was still across the back of her seat, so he stood up and grabbed it, and started making for the door when she suddenly appeared.

'Thank you,' she said and made her way back right to the corridor and over towards the car. There was now rain setting in and Ross managed to convince Clarissa to take his car. As he sped through the night, he could hear her feet tapping.

'No need to get so agitated,' said Ross.

'It's not agitation. We're close to knowing what's going on, Ross. Can you feel it?'

Ross saw something in Clarissa that was very like the boss. Macleod was all calm until he could get to that point where he could reach out, grab a case by its throat, and solve it. She was the same and maybe that was why the boss liked her. That thing beyond normal police work, that determination, that knowing when you were close, that was a feeling that Ross never got. His was the dogged determination, search and search again. He understood Hope McGrath more than Macleod, but he still admired the man for all of that. He really did have a nose for it.

As Ross pulled up in the car, Clarissa jumped from it and walked briskly up to the front door of a house. As she was about to press the doorbell, she turned back to Ross.

'Forty-seven, wasn't it? This is the right one?'

'Yes,' said Ross. 'Forty-seven.'

She turned and jabbed the doorbell with her finger. The door opened and a man with greying hair answered the door.

'My name is DS Clarissa Urquhart. This is DC Alan Ross and we're here to ask you some questions, Mr. Thomas.'

'Yes, they said you'd be coming. Not a problem. Do you want to come in?'

'By all means,' said Clarissa, and she was led through to a cosy living room with a fire blazing. The man pointed to two seats on one side and sat down in an armchair before a rather rotund woman appeared at the door behind them.

'Tea? Do you want some biscuits?'

'I'm fine,' said Clarissa. 'We probably won't be too long. We just need to know some details.'

'But thank you,' said Ross. 'Very kind.'

'Mr. Thomas,' said Clarissa, 'you remember a patient called Moira Gladstone?'

The man nodded. 'Aye, I do. You see, Moira was a bit of a case. She committed suicide in the night. She wasn't happy about something that happened in Africa.'

'Where in Africa specifically?' asked Ross.

'I think it was the Congo, back in her day. We traced it round to the sixties, probably the early part. Sometimes she wasn't too clear, but I was with her for such a long time, you learn to pick things up. From what I can gather, she was a worker out there with the tribespeople. There was a lot of civil war, certainly trouble going on and it seemed that one tribe attacked the other, wiping them out.'

'And this affected her?' said Clarissa.

'Oh, badly. You see, she wasn't there for it. This is what she said to me, she wasn't there for it. She lost them all. She worked with them, worked with the kids especially, that was

188

what got her. She said that he never protected the kids. In fact, he gave the kids up.'

'He?'

'Yes, he. We never got the full name of who it was. Danny, that's the only thing she ever said was Danny. "Danny gave them up." I mean, we tried to ask further who it was, more out of just interest than anything else, and maybe we could have picked up the full story from him if he was still around, but she said he left the kids. Handed them over. It was all pretty shocking. In one sense, you wanted to try and talk her through it and help her with it. On the other, you were sitting, thinking, "Maybe she needs to go and think about something else" but it grated on her for years and years. We stopped her three times from committing suicide. Isla was a lovely woman. She really was quite caring. Never wanted to harm a soul, but her daughter, she was the one who was particularly livid about it.'

'How do you mean?' asked Clarissa.

'Well, you see, Isla was upset, in turmoil with it. She felt that she let down the children by being away, but she was pregnant, had gone off to have the baby. I got the impression Danny and her were an item of some sort, although I'm not sure if in those days that was seen as a good thing. They certainly weren't married from what I could gather. He had promised her about marriage or something and then this all happened and Danny wasn't there, and Danny was this, Danny was that. Certainly, we never saw Danny in her life around the home.'

'But you said she was eaten up by it. She was the one suffering from it, but you were mentioning somebody was different?'

'Her daughter,' said Mr. Thomas. 'I mean, I saw her daughter a lot, but she got more and more angry over the years. Bitter, really bitter. I was actually worried for her as well. She needed to get her mental health checked, but you can't help somebody like that unless they ask. She wasn't showing any outward signs that you could approach her with other than just being really upset by it and you couldn't blame her for that, could you? After all, her mother was trying to commit suicide over this incident. Maybe Danny was her father. Maybe she wanted to get to him, anger at him. It's just a mess, really, isn't it?'

Ross nodded, but he noticed Clarissa was staring off into the fire.

'Do you have any idea where this woman lived?'

'Which one?' asked Mr. Thomas.

'Either,' said Ross quickly.

'Well, obviously, Isla lived with us for a number of years in a special home. I don't know any addresses of where she was before. But the daughter, she lived in one of the islands. She moved out there not that long ago.'

'Which island?' asked Ross. 'It is important.'

The man sat back in the chair, thinking. 'The inner ones. The inner ones below Skye. Rùm? Eigg? One of those ones.'

Ross looked at Clarissa and Clarissa turned to the man. 'You ever heard the name Margaret McCormack?'

'Never. Never heard of it.'

'Would you be able to describe the daughter Moira?'

Clarissa listened as the description came through, noting down every detail from the black hair to the rough size and the frame of the woman.

'Can you excuse me a second?' said Clarissa and turned to Ross, announcing she was going to phone Macleod. As she left the room, Thomas turned to Ross, asking, 'Have I been of any help?'

    'Oh, absolutely. Absolutely, sir.'

Chapter 22

'Seoras,' said Clarissa, 'get your pen and write down this description. Tell me if it fits anyone you know.'

Macleod felt a little bit uppity at this guessing game from Clarissa, but he wrote down the description he was handed and began thinking through the residents at the home.

'It's nobody that lives here,' said Macleod.

'Think wider,' said Clarissa. Macleod started thinking of Janey Smart, and then the other women that were around the place. 'Moira,' said Macleod. 'Moira Hunter, the counsellor?'

'Yes. Apparently, her real name's Gladstone. Her mother was also out in the Congo. If you ask Daniel, you'll find out he had an affair with her of some sort. She had a baby. Isla Gladstone had a baby. That's why she wasn't there when the tragedy happened. Moira is that baby. Isla committed suicide in a home a number of years ago, not that long, maybe about four. It seems that there's a grand plan being hatched by Moira to get them all. I think she blames them for her mother's death.'

'And she's got them here. How?'

'She's Margaret McCormack. She's the woman who first gave the idea. That's why this frontman isn't around anymore.

Kieran Jones, who put up Smart Construction as a front ahead of himself, he then got Alexander Cheshire to pretend to be him. I think Moira has done away with him. That's why there was all this detail about going off to Canada and not having spoken to Janey for a while. Moira's your woman. She's killing them.'

'But how?' said Macleod. 'How is she killing them? She's just a counsellor. She's just a . . .' And he stopped himself.

'It does seem a little far-fetched, doesn't it?'

'I don't rule anything out,' said Macleod. 'You don't think she's able to twist them in some way? I mean, have some sort of skill that mind control or some sort of—'

'Kieran,' said Clarissa. 'Kieran said it. Kieran said that when he first met her at the Refugees of War fundraiser that her father, her father was doing a hypnotism act.'

'Hypnotism?' said Macleod.

'So, she'd be able to somehow control them. She might have learned it off him. I mean, she'd have perfect access to them, wouldn't she?'

'That she would, Clarissa. That she would. I think you and Ross have got it. Blast, and she's had access to them all this time. She'd have access to them. She could implant in them, tell them to go and do this, hypnotise them to do it. They wouldn't even realise it. And of course, it'll be perfectly normal for them to talk to her about problems, about what they'd had in the past. She's influenced the whole thing. She's brought them all together.'

'Shall I get some people sent over to you?'

'You'll not get them tonight. It's wild down here,' said Macleod. 'I'm trying to establish some sort of a curfew in the home. That's why they just disappear off one at a time.

193

They just make a runner, and they have no idea what they're doing.'

'But what happened to Hope's aunt?' said Clarissa. 'She had an arm chopped off. How does that work?'

'I don't know. I don't care at the moment. I need to get somebody on that woman, and I need somebody up here to stay and watch. Ross and you, get down to Oban so you can get the next boat out here as soon as.'

'We're on our way, Seoras, but if it's as rough as you said is, it could be morning before we're there.'

'I don't care. Get on the move. I'll call you back when I understand if we've got her or not.'

Macleod placed his mobile away and scanned the room looking for Hope. He saw her in the far corner and shouted, 'McGrath, come here now.'

Hope saw the urgency in her boss's eyes and briskly walked across. Together they sat down, huddled close. 'What's up, Seoras?' she asked.

'It's Moira, the counsellor,' he said and related what Clarissa had just told him.

'Do you really think she can have that much influence?' asked Hope.

'You explain what's happening here then,' he said. 'People are just leaping off. This is either mass hysteria or somebody is in the minds of these people.'

'When was the last time she spoke to them?' asked Hope.

'She has had restricted access with all that's going on. I mean, we didn't turn around and say she can't come. She's the nurse. She needs to look after them. She's still been attending to their other needs,' said Macleod. 'She could have been talking to them all along.'

194

He turned and saw Angusina in the corner. 'Angusina,' he said, approaching her, 'when was the last time you saw the counsellor? When did you last see the nurse, Moira?'

'Yesterday,' said Angusina.

'And what did she talk to you about?'

'Well, that's private, isn't it?' said Angusina. 'I also had to take some pills. That's on my medical sheet. You'll see that. Janey has to know about that, but the other stuff we talk about, that's private.'

Macleod frowned. It was indeed private, but he needed to know. 'Did she in any way seem strange to you?' asked Macleod.

'No. She's very helpful. She is very helpful.'

As he turned away, Hope whispered in his ear. 'Very helpful. She's got three bloody suicides. Four now, actually. How can you have any sort of track record like that?'

'Just a moment,' said Macleod. He looked over and saw Sheila and made his way over to her. 'Sheila,' asked Macleod, 'when was the last time you saw Moira, the counsellor?'

'Yesterday,' said Sheila. 'And what did you talk about at your appointment?' he asked. 'That's private,' said Sheila. 'You can't ask that, but I had my medication. I mean, Janey's got all that if you need it.'

Macleod frowned but said thank you. He turned and looked again. He saw Jake moping on a seat and made his way over. 'You ask him,' Macleod said to Hope. Kneeling down, she got into the face of Jake.

'Jake,' said Hope gently, 'can I ask you something?' The man nodded. 'When was the last time you saw Moira, the counsellor?'

'Yesterday,' he said.

195

'And what did you talk about?'

'That would be private,' said Jake. 'I did get my medication. Janey's seen to that. Janey knows all about it.'

'Okay. I take it she was helping you with your grief over losing your wife.'

'That would be private,' he said.

'It's a hard time,' said Hope. 'I mean, you need to talk about it. I guess that's the sort of thing she would have said to you.'

'That would be private,' said Jake. Hope thanked the man and stood up walked away with Macleod.

'That would be private. That's all we get from them,' said Macleod. 'That would be private. It's the same damn words. Somebody messed with their mind and everything's pointing to her. I need you to go and put her under arrest despite this storm. There's not going to be an easy way to get her out but she can't be near these people again. She can't; otherwise, who knows what she could do. We can't spook her either. We can't arrive on force.'

'We haven't got a force,' said Hope. 'It's you and me the way this weather is.'

'And I don't want to leave this long,' said Macleod. 'If she's got in their heads who knows who's going to walk out on that path next? I mean, Hope, they all signed the book on the way out before they jumped.'

Macleod could see the anger rising in Hope. 'Easy, McGrath. Easy. You can't take this personal.'

'How the hell am I not meant to take it personally? This woman murdered my aunt!'

'She'll pay for it,' said Macleod. 'She'll pay for it, but we have to do it right. You have to do it right. You can't go in with that face. She'll know something's up.'

'Okay, Seoras, okay. Why don't you go and get her?'

'Because you can handle yourself. If she has somebody with her, I haven't got a hope. Look at me, McGrath. Look at me. What age am I now? Yes, I run around, but there's no way I can handle someone like that. If Stewart was here I'd send her, but you can handle yourself just as well. Go and arrest her. Keep her quiet.'

'Okay. I'll take the car, drive down, and then I'll bring her back up here. We can stick her in one of the rooms. It's best the two of us are not apart throughout the night. Got to watch each other's back till this storm comes through, until we can get more bodies out here and resolve this properly.'

'Agreed,' said Macleod. 'But be careful. She's not daft. You see what she's done here. And be careful in case she hypnotises you. Don't give her a chance to say a lot.'

'How do you think she hypnotises people?' asked Hope. 'What should I look out for?'

'How would I know? I suggest you don't let her speak much. Get close to her. Keep your eyes off her though. I think that's how they say it's done, isn't it? A lot through the eyes.'

Hope looked at Macleod. 'You really haven't got a clue how this works, do you?'

'Neither do you, so we need to tread carefully. I'm hoping it takes her time and hopefully it takes her one of those meetings to sit and talk to somebody to hypnotise them to this level, day after day after day. I don't think it's a snap of the fingers. I pray to God it's not a snap of the fingers, Hope, because I feel like I'm sending you into the lion's den.'

'Or we could just wait it out,' she said. 'We could just wait here with everyone.'

'No,' said Macleod. 'Because you don't know what she's up

to. You don't know how much is involved in this. Could she run? Could she activate something? Maybe she'd phone the home here and get through to one of these people and set them off. If they're hypnotised it could be done remotely.'

'You're kind of being wide ranging here,' said Hope.

'I haven't got a clue what she could do,' said Macleod. 'That's why we need to get eyes on her now. Lock her away, make sure she's access to nothing. Hope, for all I know she could activate one of these lot to come after us.'

Macleod felt helpless. He really wasn't sure what he was up against. Just what could the woman do? Was she capable of influencing these people, even at a distance? What had she done? He needed an interrogator to find out what she was up to, find out if anything else was going to happen tonight. After all, she wasn't around when they went and jumped. Were there preprogramed times? Had she set them out to do it at different intervals? Had she ramped things up, given that there were police officers at the township?

'Off you go,' said Macleod. Hope nodded.

* * *

Hope stepped out into the rain from the car, felt the wind cutting across her, but the house of Moira Hunter was directly in front of her. There was a light on in the living room and Hope made her way to the front door, rapping it loudly. She felt her jeans becoming soaked already and was glad of her leather jacket keeping the rain off her. She'd let her hair down so that it soaked up the rain before it hit her neck, but as the door opened she felt a chill inside.

'Oh, Sergeant. What are you doing out here? Come on in,'

said Moira. The black-haired woman looked as if she was some kindly soul bringing a waif in out of the rain. Hope stepped in carefully, looking around a quiet hall. 'Straight through. There's a fire inside,' said Moira. 'You can warm yourself up.'

Hope gave her jacket a shake before stepping inside and moved close to the fire.

'Would you like a cup of tea or something?' said Moira. 'What's this about? Something happened over the home?'

'No,' said Hope. 'Were you expecting something to happen?'

'No, it's just the way this weather is. I wasn't expecting anyone to be out here. Must be something serious you've come for.'

'I need to talk to you about something,' said Hope.

'Maybe I can get you a cup of tea first,' said Moira.

Hope stepped closer to the woman. 'I'm afraid not,' she said. 'I'm afraid I'm putting you under arrest.' Hope reached forward, grabbed the woman's wrist and took her hand up behind her back. She began to read her rights to the woman who stayed quiet. Hope found it eerie that she wasn't protesting, wasn't saying anything until she suddenly turned round, looking directly at Hope. Hope averted her eyes down, but the woman spoke.

'Missing anyone from the home, are we?' said Moira. 'Are they all tucked up in their beds? Is the Inspector on top of it?' Something inside Hope froze. Had she programmed them to attack Macleod? Was she now in the wrong place?

'I wonder, has he noticed yet? They come in and out of their rooms, don't they? Those posh rooms, the ones that have the beds and sofas. A house, a house in a room, really, isn't it? With the breath-taking views. Oh, I sold that well, didn't I? I sold that well and got them to come here. And then when they came here, I held them in my hand. I am impressed though, Sergeant. I'm impressed that you found me out. Very impressed. I'm just a little disappointed. Especially in your Inspector. Are you not going to ask why?'

Hope remained silent, determined not to give the woman anything.

'You see, if he'd done a count, and I know it's easy to miss, but he might have wondered where Daniel was.' Hope heard something behind her, turned around, and saw a block of wood come down on her head. Everything went black.

Chapter 23

Hope groaned. Her head was ringing, and she remembered the block of wood that Daniel had swung at her head. She reached up to feel the cut under her hair and then brought her hand in front of her face. She could see blood on her fingertips.

She wondered how long she'd been out for, and then a terror struck her. Macleod was on his own up at the home. Was Moira on the move? What would she do? Obviously, Hope wasn't a target, for she wasn't dead, instead just simply left after being battered. She felt a bruise on her ribs and realised she must have been kicked after she'd been knocked out. Slowly she rolled over and scanned the room for a clock. The fire was dying low. As she gazed over she saw it said 3:30 a.m. on the face of a small gold carriage clock on the mantlepiece.

The time—3:30 a.m.—that means they would have been gone nearly three hours. Hope raised herself and reached for her mobile, but it was missing. As she stood, she felt groggy, put her hand out to stop herself from tumbling over and took a moment to just steady. Her sight was slightly blurry at the edges, but it was coming into focus, although with the darkness of the room it was hard to tell just how sharp her sight was.

But she'd seen the clock face.

Hope reached up again to the back of her head and examined her wound with her fingers. Clearly, she wasn't bleeding out, because, although the blood she touched was fresh, there didn't appear to be a lot of it spilling out. Then she saw on the floor beside her a cloth that was red with blood. Maybe it was her blood. Maybe somebody had tried to stop the flow. Hope didn't know, and at the moment she didn't care. Her first thought was Macleod and the residents up at the home who had to be warned.

She staggered out of the room into the hall, opened the front door to see the driving rain, and felt the wind whip past her hair. It was cold, that autumnal chill that you got but she'd be all right for the car was outside. It would take her up to the home in no time. But it wasn't there.

Hope looked around desperately but her car was gone. She felt inside her pocket and realised there were no keys. *Oh hell*, she thought. This was no night for running up through small roads exposed to the rain and the wind, but Seoras needed her. He needed to be warned. Maybe he knew by now because she wasn't back. She shut the door briefly, gathered her strength, and began looking around for a jacket of some sort. Under the stairs, she saw a Kagool but when she tried it on, she couldn't make her shoulders fit and it just felt restrictive. Instead she zipped up her leather jacket and found a piece of material to tie up her hair behind her. She was going to get soaked anyway so she might as well not have her red mop flying across her face in the wind.

As she opened the door, she fought back ideas that Macleod might be under attack, that he could be in serious trouble. There was also a brief thought about why she had been spared.

Had he thought her dead? Had somebody put a cloth on her head? But there was no time to think. There was only time to do, and Hope stepped out into the wind and rain and shut the door behind her.

She looked up to the left where the road departed from the house. Stumbling along, she got to the end of this particular section and found the road turning left or right. Moira's house was away from the main settlements on Eigg, although to call them settlements was exaggerating it a bit. There were maybe two or three houses together in places but Moira's was away from everyone. Hope tried to work out in her head how far it would be to run to the other homes and get a lift to the retirement township. Or would she be better simply running straight to it? She couldn't think, the pain in her head pounding her again and again. 'The township was left. The township was left,' she kept saying to herself. Left it was. Hope staggered off into the night.

* * *

Macleod looked at his clock and wondered where Hope was. He expected to hear from her, at least a phone call. The weather had got worse and maybe she'd thought about not driving up. Or maybe it would be hard to take the woman out to the car securely and she was just staying put, but whatever, he'd expected a phone call. Had things gone awry?

He didn't know but what he was aware of now was that Daniel Edwards did not seem to be in the home. Angusina had mentioned it and Macleod had instantly gone over to the daybook that the residents signed when they left the building, but his name wasn't there. Macleod had stared along the path up to the singing sands. Again, there was nothing. To go outside would surely be folly, and besides, there was plenty more of the residents in the township that he needed to keep hold of.

He tried his mobile to ring Hope several times and it rang out until her answer message kicked in. Whatever had happened to her, she wasn't picking up. His stomach was twisting tighter and tighter into a knot of fear. Despite all his years of police work, he still got afraid. He still realised the people he was working against were killers. Most of the time they weren't trying to kill him, he was simply the guy following them, tidying up after them, putting them behind bars, but now his sergeant was in trouble.

He had gathered the rest of the residents into the common room and at this hour of half three, a number of them were asleep. Angusina was in the corner knitting but Sheila and Dennis, the clothing gurus, were stretched out together on one of the sofas. Jake was asleep as well. Macleod also had Janey Smart tucked away in a guest room, locked in with a key only he possessed. He wasn't sure how much she knew, if the killer needed her to be dispatched, but knowing now that her father was also staying clear of the area because of the killer, his apprehension about her was strong.

Blast this weather, he thought. *If it hadn't have been for this weather, I could have had people all over here. We'd have this done in no time. We've got Moira, after all. We just haven't got a hold of her. Then all the psych doctors or whoever could come in and prove what they'd done. Show the conditioning or however it worked.*

Macleod was more used to straightforward murders. People took weapons and killed people, or they shoved them off cliffs or poisoned them. These were things he could handle. This idea that somebody could hypnotise, get hold of someone mentally, and torture them before getting them to kill themselves was a new one on him, but the idea wasn't ridiculous. He'd seen those hypnotists, he'd seen people stand up and pretend they were babies, had seen a man stand in front of them, shouting at Macleod to get out of a room because it was flooding. Why couldn't you tell someone children were coming for them? Why couldn't you tap into those memories? Why couldn't you tell them to leap, throw themselves to the sea? After all, it didn't have to be the sea to them, did it?

Macleod saw a set of lights out in the car park, flashing several times. They were held on for a second, then off, then held on for another second, then flashed quickly four times, then held on for another second, and for another time. He saw Angusina move over to the windows that looked out onto the car park. She then turned and almost fell over Jake, waking him in the process.

'Just stay back from the window,' said Macleod.

'There's somebody out there,' said Angusina. 'Jake needs to see.'

'No, he doesn't,' said Macleod, but Angusina has gone over and woken Sheila and Dennis. Macleod was holding Jake back, but he had failed to stop him from seeing the lights, and then Dennis and Sheila stood up and looked. Dennis was peering past Macleod and the light sequence continued time and again.

Macleod was unsure what to do. He needed to stop it, so he made his way out into the entrance hallway, then opened the doors. He saw a figure in the car, but the car was the one Hope had driven away in. He had seen her take it down to Moira's. Quickly he ran over, but the lights were now dark, and when he got there and opened the car door, no one was inside. He tensed up and ran back into the retirement home.

From the hallway, he couldn't see anyone in the common room, but the door at the far end was open. He had been outside less than a minute, but now Angusina, Sheila, and Dennis were gone. Jake was missing as well, and Macleod saw the door out to the singing sounds path being shut by him. He then saw Dennis and Sheila lift some sort of bench, putting it in front of the door, and with that, they turned and were off, not exactly running, but walking as briskly as they could, up along the ill-fated path.

They were out now and Macleod was on his own. Did he race out into the dark? Who had been flashing the lights? Was Moira out there on the loose as well? He needed backup. He needed somebody with him.

From the entrance hall, he ran to the office suite and found the room where Janey Smart was locked in. He thundered on the door, unlocked it, and as he opened it, the woman was standing up.

'What's up, Inspector? What's the matter?'

'They've all gone, Janey. They've all gone up the singing sands path. I need you with me.'

'Why?' she asked. 'What are they doing?'

'I don't know. It's Moira. Moira is the one doing this.'

'Moira is their nurse. How could Moira do it?'

'I think she knows hypnotism. Her mother was with them out in the Congo. Daniel is her father. Come on. We need to go.' Macleod was getting stroppy with Janey, but he realised that the poor girl didn't understand fully what was happening, so he reached forward, grabbed her hand, and pulled her out of the room with him. When they reached the common room, he ran over to the door that was blocked by the furniture outside.

'Give me a hand,' he said, 'give me a hand to open this.'

Janey, however, was by the book. 'They've all signed it, Inspector.'

Macleod's heart sank. *Was this some end game? Was Moira taking them all down in one?*

'Give me a hand,' said Macleod. 'Let's get this open.' He shoved at the door, but it was stuck solid. The bench had been braced with other outdoor furniture around it.

'This way, Inspector. I'll get you out there quickly, but this way.' Janey disappeared along a corridor. Macleod followed past tumble dryers and sinks, and then ran out a door where the path was some fifty meters off to the left.

'This way, Inspector, keep going.' Macleod could barely see the ground under his feet, but as he reached the path, the clouds broke slightly, and moonlight was cast down. He could see the sea out in the distance, endless shades of a dark mass that spat up here and there, a rollicking surface that didn't seem to end. Ahead of him, the path continued to swing on, while down below he could see the sands.

'We've got to keep going,' said Macleod. 'Keep going, Janey.' Together they ran, head into the wind. Macleod had his coat on, but Janey had been dressed just in a T-shirt and jeans, and he could see the woman getting cold as she ran.

Upon the path ahead, Macleod saw a figure. It stood around average height and he swore there was a snarl on the face. It wasn't fully distinct, but he reckoned it was Moira. What was distinct was the blade in her hand. The little moonlight that there was glinted off it. Macleod looked down on the beach and could see several of the residents running forward. Up ahead, he saw Daniel Edwards beyond him, climbing up onto the protective railing, where the cliffs looked down towards the singing sands.

'You're too late, Inspector,' said Moira. 'I don't want to kill you, but I will. And this lot are going to their doom.'

'Put the weapon down,' said Macleod, as he got closer and realised it was not a simple knife, but rather a machete. 'Put that away.'

'Poetic, isn't it? A machete. Did you know that they took an arm off a child? Mary McGrath held that child. They took an arm off him. That's why she was missing an arm. They're getting their comeuppance, Inspector. They killed my mother, and that man behind me, he saw to her doom.'

'That's your father,' shouted Macleod. 'That is your father. Your mother was having relations with him. It's only reason you're alive. She went. You realise, that don't you? She wasn't there only because of you.'

'She would have died with those children. Anybody of right mind would have died with them, and because of that, she was wracked with guilt for years, wracked with guilt. Well, I've wracked them with guilt, and now they're going to die too by their own hand.'

Macleod took off his coat, realizing he needed to get to Daniel quickly but the large blade in front of him was very real. He wrapped his coat in front of him, making his way forward, but he shouted over to Janey.

'Get down onto the beach. See if you can stop the others going in the water.'

'What about you?' said Janey. 'She'll kill you.'

'No, she won't,' said Macleod. 'You stop those people. That's your job but don't go out of your depth; keep yourself safe too.'

Hopefully, if he sent Janey that way, Moira wouldn't do anything to her. Macleod looked ahead and with the coat before him, he rushed at Moira. She slashed down and he put his arms up so the blade caught the coat. He tried to wrap her hand in it, but she pushed forward, and he tumbled back, losing the grip on his coat, falling down to the floor. She threw the coat aside, picked up her machete, and yelled at him.

'I don't want to do this to you. All you've got to do stay there. You hear me, Inspector? Just stay there.' Macleod pushed himself up onto his backside to try to stand up. Moira kicked him in the face, and he fell backwards, smacking his head on the path. It was like the world was spinning but as his eyes refocused, he saw Moira's face above him.

'All you had to do was stay still. All you had to do was get out of the way, but I can't let anything stop me. You understand that?' She lifted the machete up with her right arm and went to bring it down on Macleod. He threw his hands up in front of him, unable to do anything else.

Something went quickly over the top of him. It clattered into Moira, knocking her down off her feet. Macleod heard the machete bounce off along the path. As he pushed himself back up, the world still spinning, he saw the red hair of Hope McGrath and saw her fist coming down from her height, twice. Then she stood up and turned to him.

'Seoras, are you okay?'

'Get him,' he shouted. 'Get him.'

With that, Hope turned and saw Daniel now standing fully on top of the railings. He was just letting his hands go, looking like an angel, arms outstretched.

'Don't,' shouted Macleod and he saw Hope run towards him.

The man shouted to the air, 'I hear the children, I hear them coming. I hear them.' With that, he pitched himself forward. Macleod saw Hope run to the railing and look down.

'The tide's right in, Seoras, the tide's right in.'

'No, Hope, don't.' The leather jacket was off. She jumped up on top of the railings and Macleod saw her take a dive. Groggily, he got his feet and managed to stagger over to the railings and look down. In the sea, he saw two heads bobbing about, but they came and went in the gloom. He turned back and saw the machete laying on the ground. Moira was beginning to move, so he ran over to her, turned her over and put her onto her front. Slapping cuffs on her, he pulled her across and put one arm behind the railings and locked the cuffs through them so that she couldn't move. He then took the machete and threw it a distance away.

'I'll be back for you,' he shouted at her but the woman didn't seem to be very aware. Hope must have hit her hard. Macleod staggered over to the steps that led down to the singing sands. Jake was crying about the children, shouting out to everyone who could hear. Ahead, Sheila and Dennis were hand in hand, stepping out into the sea. Angusina was some twenty yards ahead of them. Macleod ran forward, pitching here and there as he did so, but an outstretched hand grabbed Sheila's shoulder. His other hand grabbed the shoulder of Dennis.

'This way,' he shouted. 'The children are this way.' The couple looked at him, somewhat bemused, but he continued. 'The children are this way.' He dragged them over towards Janey and said to them, 'Sit, sit and wait for the children.'

They sat down, looking at him. 'When are they coming? We can hear them.'

'They're coming soon, but they won't come until I come back. Wait here.' He turned to Janey. 'Don't let them move, even if you have to knock them out. Whatever you do, don't let them move.'

Macleod turned and looked out to sea. He took off his suit jacket, throwing it on the floor and then ran out into the water, his eyes fixed on Angusina. The woman was up to her neck and Macleod was thankful he was a good five inches taller. As he waded out, he felt the chill of the sea running through him, the water seeping through his shirt, his body encompassed in it.

'I'm coming,' she shouted, 'I hear the children, I'm coming.'

Macleod yelled over the waves. 'This way, the children are this way,' he shouted, but Angusina kept walking.

'He knows my sin,' she shouted. 'He knows my sin.'

'You must face it,' said Macleod.

'I can't,' she yelled. When she turned and looked at him, Macleod realised that she wasn't hypnotised. 'I know my mind, Inspector,' she said. 'I know what she's done to us. She couldn't hypnotise me, I was immune.'

'You didn't tell anyone? You knew what she was doing to you?'

'I am at fault, Inspector.'

'But you'll be a suicide!' shouted Macleod. 'You can't. You know the Book doesn't allow for that.' His own feelings were being put aside. He was using everything he knew about the woman's faith to stop her, but he saw the look in the eyes and knew he was going to fail.

'I'm sorry, Inspector. Maybe they can live with it, but I won't be able to.' With that she dropped her head under the water. Macleod dove out, reaching here and there. His feet were still touching the sand below and he started to try and drag himself back in. Looking around, he saw Hope swimming strongly.

'I've got him,' shouted Hope. 'I've got him.' As she came close by him, she dragged Daniel Edwards closer to the beach until

211

he was out of the water.

'She's out there,' said Macleod turning to Hope. 'Angusina's out there.'

Hope turned to look at the sea and Macleod saw her begin to shake from the cold. The woman looked exhausted. From the side of her head, he could see fresh blood pouring.

'Your head.'

'They hit me when I was down at Moira's. It's opened up in the sea, but I'll get her,' said Hope. 'I'll get her.'

Macleod looked out to the water. There was no sign of Angusina. As Hope went to run out to the sea he stepped across. 'No,' he said. 'You're in no condition. We can't see her. She could be anywhere out there. The sea could have taken her. You're exhausted. You might not come back.'

'But I'll get her, Seoras,' said Hope. 'I'll get her.'

'She's gone, Hope. She couldn't live with her guilt. We'll let her die with it. Maybe God's more forgiving than she thinks.'

Chapter 24

'Are you ready?'

Hope stood on the singing sands path, looking out across skies that were blue, and feeling the autumnal sun on her skin. It was four days since the dramatic events at the beach and teams have been over to bag up all the evidence and take Moira Hunter away. Before she'd gone, there'd been further questioning, and Macleod had noticed that Hope had struggled with it. At the time, she felt it was personal and Macleod had excused her from a lot of the interview, bringing Clarissa in. Instead, he had prayed that the reassuring face of Ross would've been able to steady Hope, but there was an uneasiness in his sergeant that he knew couldn't remain.

'Just about,' said Hope.

'We need to get moving for the ferry soon. Doesn't come by here that often.'

'Okay, Seoras, okay. She's still out there though. Isn't she?'

'Your aunt?' said Macleod. 'The body of your aunt is out there somewhere.'

'That's what I mean. You think she'll ever surface again?'

'You know as well as I do, a lot do, a few don't. But she's not the only one at the moment. A lot of her fellow residents out there, too.'

'We did save quite a few though, didn't we?'

'We did, and I've commended you for the rescue of Daniel Edwards. Although it was one heck of a rash act.'

'You should recommend yourself. You got the rest of them back. All except Angusina.' Hope turned and faced Macleod. 'Does it haunt you, not getting her?'

'No,' said Macleod. 'Angusina wasn't hypnotised. Unlike the rest of them that Moira had hypnotised, it didn't work on Angusina. She genuinely bore the guilt. Maybe the situation brought it on more, seeing everyone again. She couldn't live with herself. I think that's why she went with the others. When those lights flashed, she knew something was up. She joined them.'

'I didn't think people from your part of the world did guilt. I thought that was the Catholics.'

'Oh, don't believe it,' said Macleod. 'We can do guilt better than the rest of them. But I feel no guilt about her death. I did what I could. I was sad, still am sad about it, but I don't feel guilt. It's not your aunt that bothers you, though, is it?'

'Well, not just my aunt.'

Macleod stepped forward to put his arm around Hope. 'I did my best to reach Nancy,' she said. 'Now every time I look, I see Jake. Everyone else has come out of the hypnotism, starting their deprogramming, and they appear to be happy about it, but Jake's not. He lost everything.'

'She was probably dead by the time you got near her. She would have been in the water for quite a while. You can't blame yourself for that.'

'You think I should make some sort of grave for her? Some

sort of reminder, somewhere?'

'For your aunt?' said Macleod. 'There's one here.'

'It's just an empty box. An empty box in a place that was not her home.'

'Where would you put it?' asked Macleod. 'What's the point of it? If it's for you, put it near you, but you don't need somewhere to go to unless you want it. Just speak.'

'I didn't think I'd hear that from you. You think the dead can hear us?'

Macleod shrugged his shoulders. 'I could give you all the theology,' he said, 'but it'd be pretty pointless, because no one really knows for sure. No one knows if they watch us. No one knows if they disappear into the earth. No one knows if there's nothing. No one knows. We only have what we believe. If it helps you, talk to her. If it helps you to have somewhere to go to remember her, make something. I know what I believe, Hope, but I'm past the days of forcing it on everyone else.'

She turned and hugged him. 'Sometimes you're a darn good friend. Do you know that?' she said. 'Sometimes you feel like my closest friend.'

'Your closest friend's waiting for you. Just let him finish up getting the hire cars out. Then he'll be ready for you.'

Hope dug her elbow into Macleod. 'You have to stop calling him Car-Hire-Man.'

'Well,' said Macleod, 'it's what he does. Besides, it wasn't me that started that.'

'Is that why you brought Clarissa in, to just get more jabs? You couldn't handle what I was saying to you?'

Macleod stared off out into the sea. 'That's exactly right,' he said. 'I pick all my colleagues on the basis that I can't defend myself. Now get going. I'll see you in the car.'

Macleod watched Hope walk off. She was wearing the black leather jacket that she'd flung into the air before diving in off the singing sands path, and as he watched her go, he realised there was tremendous pride in him, for from the early days of having seen her as some sort of brazen woman, he now saw her as—well, what did he see? Well, he saw a heck of a detective. And she was right. A friend. They were friends. He noticed her wave to someone. Then he saw the scarf billowing from the woman's neck, a large shawl flung round her, and an attitude he could feel from a distance.

'Are we all wrapped up, Clarissa?' he asked.

'All done, Seoras. You did well here.'

'I wasn't aware that I'd solicited any suggestions from you about how we'd done.'

'Don't get cute on me. You know you did well.'

'We wouldn't have got to the bottom of it without you, you and Ross. I think you work well together.'

'Well, you always like the younger woman with you, don't you?'

Macleod gave a glare. 'I wouldn't take that insubordination from other people. You do realise that.'

Clarissa put her hand up to her eyes and looked out into the sea. 'Are you okay?'

'What do you mean?' asked Macleod.

'I asked if you're okay. The younger ones, Hope, Ross, they see you as some sort of tower of strength. Somebody who doesn't get affected by things, can stand there making the decisions. They wonder how you can be so devoid of an emotional reaction at times.'

'And you don't see me like that?'

'No, I've got your number,' said Clarissa. Macleod saw the

grin on her face.

'No, I'm not all right,' he said, 'but Jane gets to hear about that. She wanted in when we first met and for a time, I kept her out, but not now. Now she hears about it.'

'If there's ever anything you can't tell her and you need someone from the force,' said Clarissa, 'you know you can speak to me. Us old dogs need to stick together.'

'And what?' said Macleod. 'You won't have a cheeky word? You won't take the mick out of me?'

'Oh, I'll do that, all right,' said Clarissa. 'But if you need someone, I'm here. I know you find me strange, Seoras, but I'm here.' Macleod nodded. Clarissa turned away and began to walk.

Macleod shouted after, 'Urquhart, I don't find you strange, contrary to popular opinion. I think I understand you perfectly. Why do you think you're here?'

She didn't even cast her head back, just kept walking and Macleod felt he could see the smile on her face. He turned away from the path and walked back towards the retirement township, entering through the door into the common room that the residents had run out of only four nights ago. Janey Smart was there talking to the residents, and she approached Macleod as he stepped inside the building.

'Thank you, Inspector. I know when you locked me up, it was for my own protection, though you didn't tell me. My father's been in touch. He wanted me to pass on his thanks to you, and especially to Clarissa.'

'You mean DS Urquhart,' said Macleod, pulling his formal face.

'No,' said Janey. 'It's Clarissa. I think he knows her from before. They might have been an item at one point.' Macleod pulled a face.

'Just glad to see that you're okay,' he said. 'It's all wrapped up. I hope you can make the business work, get some ordinary people in here. A peaceful place with no agenda behind it.'

'Well, I'll do my best. The thing is, with all the suicides, it'll make the press. Some people love that, don't they? I might have to capitalize on it.'

Macleod didn't like that idea, but he simply nodded and shook Janey's hand. 'Thank you for all your efforts on that night.'

'And thank you for taking on the mad machete-wielding woman,' said Janey. 'I thought you were quite gruff when you were here. Very stern, but when I saw you step in front of me, there was no way you were going to let me protect you, was there?'

'That's my job,' said Macleod, and he shook hands and walked out to the front of the building. He saw Clarissa drive off with Hope in the car. Other police cars were drifting away, but at the front of the building sat Ross with the door open for the Inspector. He stepped inside, closed the door, and turned to his faithful constable.

'We wouldn't have got here without you, Ross. I need to get you somebody extra. I need you to go and find someone who understands about this computer stuff. Someone who can work in the office to give you a hand. Can you do that for me?'

'Of course, sir. Of course, I can.'

'And I need you to do a little background checking for me. You went to see Kieran Jones and got the information from him. Did he and Sergeant Urquhart seem to develop a rapport?'

'A rapport, sir? No. A fine officer she is. She doesn't say a word out of line, treated him as a gentleman, nothing else.'

'His daughter seemed to think that Sergeant Urquhart knew the man quite well.'

'I must have missed that, sir.'

Ross started the car and drove out of the car park, taking the small roads down towards the ferry terminal. As they were approaching, Macleod turned to him again. 'Are you sure she didn't know Kieran Jones?'

'Not that I'm aware of, sir. True professional. Glad you brought her on board.'

'You realise how bad you are at lying, don't you, Ross? I mean, you don't have to do it to my face.'

'And you really don't need to ask those questions, sir,' he said. Macleod jolted and stared across at Ross.

'You've never said something like that to me,' he said. 'In all our time together, you would never have dared.'

'Well, no, sir. But some people would say it was your fault.'

'My fault?' said Macleod. He waited for Ross to tell him about the difficult situation Macleod had put him in, but instead, the man just nodded.

'Yes, sir. It's your fault. You paired me up with Urquhart. It wasn't my choice.' Macleod turned away to look out the window and began to chortle inadvertently to himself. Clarissa was having an effect on the team, and he thought it was a good one. As he approached the ferry, he got out to see Hope waiting to get on board.

'Okay?'

'Okay,' said Hope. A voice from beside them shouted over. 'Of course, she's okay. Car-Hire-Man will probably be on the other side.'

'He's not Car-Hire-Man,' said Hope.

'Well, he is Car-Hire-Man.'

'Clarissa,' said Macleod. 'Stop teasing. He's got a name.'

'Oh, yes, Car-Hire-Man's got a name,' said Clarissa. 'What is it, Seoras?'

In the next ten seconds of silence, Macleod saw Hope's eyes narrow on him, but his mind went blank. 'Okay,' said Macleod, 'Car-Hire-Man will be waiting.' He felt the punch on his shoulder from Hope.

Read on to discover the Patrick Smythe series!

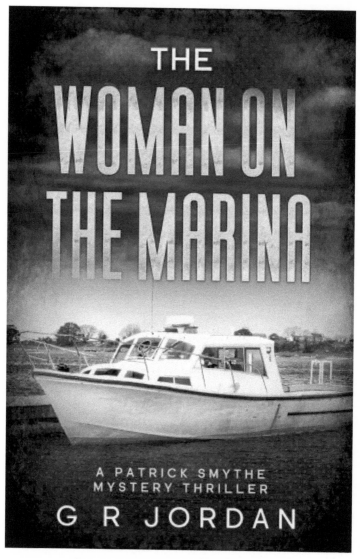

Start your Patrick Smythe journey here!

Patrick Smythe is a former Northern Irish policeman who

after suffering an amputation after a bomb blast, takes to the sea between the west coast of Scotland and his homeland to ply his trade as a private investigator. Join Paddy as he tries to work to his own ethics while knowing how to bend the rules he once enforced. Working from his beloved motorboat 'Craigantlet', Paddy decides to rescue a drug mule in this short story from the pen of G R Jordan.

Join G R Jordan's monthly newsletter about forthcoming releases and special writings for his tribe of avid readers and then receive your free Patrick Smythe short story.

Go to https://bit.ly/PatrickSmythe for your Patrick Smythe journey to start!

About the Author

GR Jordan is a self-published author who finally decided at forty that in order to have an enjoyable lifestyle, his creative beast within would have to be unleashed. His books mirror that conflict in life where acts of decency contend with self-promotion, goodness stares in horror at evil, and kindness blindsides us when we at our worst. Corrupting our world with his parade of wondrous and horrific characters, he highlights everyday tensions with fresh eyes whilst taking his methodical, intelligent mainstays on a roller-coaster ride of dilemmas, all the while suffering the banter of their provocative sidekicks.

A graduate of Loughborough University where he masqueraded as a chemical engineer but ultimately played American football, Gary had worked at changing the shape of cereal flakes and pulled a pallet truck for a living. Watching vegetables freeze at -40'C was another career highlight and he was also one of the Scottish Highlands "blind" air traffic controllers.

These days he has graduated to answering a telephone to people in trouble before telephoning other people to sort it out.

Having flirted with most places in the UK, he is now based in the Isle of Lewis in Scotland where his free time is spent between raising a young family with his wife, writing, figuring out how to work a loom and caring for a small flock of chickens. Luckily, his writing is influenced by his varied work and life experience as the chickens have not been the poetical inspiration he had hoped for!

You can connect with me on:

○ https://grjordan.com

🗗 https://facebook.com/carpetlessleprechaun

Subscribe to my newsletter:

✉ https://bit.ly/PatrickSmythe

Also by G R Jordan

G R Jordan writes across multiple genres including crime, dark and action adventure fantasy, feel good fantasy, mystery thriller and horror fantasy. Below is a selection of his work. Whilst all books are available across online stores, signed copies are available at his personal shop.

Where Justice Fails (Highlands & Islands Detective Thriller #16)
https://grjordan.com/product/where-justice-fails
A disturbed grave and a switched corpse. A new TV show and a quest for the truth. Can Macleod and McGrath bring an increasingly popular vigilante to justice before mob rule takes over?

When the first episodes of a new programme coincide with the discovery of corpse switching, Macleod believes the gaudy production is merely fuelling high jinks from a disaffected community. But when the presenter becomes a spokesperson for the lack of justice, the Inspector finds his casebook increases with previously thought innocent suspects. Can the team discover the connection between the weekly show and the spate of new killings before a growing clamour for justice becomes the prelude to kangaroo courts?

Make way for the public's arbiter of justice!

The Express Wishes of Mr MacIver (Kirsten Stewart Thrillers #3)

https://grjordan.com/product/express-wishes

A scramble for diamonds on Scotland's north coast. A murderous group intent on an explosive end if disappointed. Can Kirsten prevent a catastrophe on the largest cruise ship to visit the Hebridean Isles?

In her third novel, Kirsten must use the guile and expertise of her newly formed team to prevent the largest shipping disaster ever seen in the northern waters of Scotland. With the clock ticking and a nation with its finger on the trigger, will the Inverness team find a country's missing heritage, or will they join thousands in an explosion of titanic proportions?

The cold waters of the Minch await the tardy courier!

Corpse Reviver (A Contessa Munroe Mystery #1)

https://grjordan.com/product/corspe-reviver

A widowed Contessa flees to the northern waters in search of adventure. An entrepreneur dies on an ice pack excursion. But when the victim starts moonlighting from his locked cabin, can the Contessa uncover the true mystery of his death?

Catriona Cullodena Munroe, widow of the late Count de Los Palermo, has fled the family home, avoiding the scramble for title and land. As she searches for the life she always wanted, the Contessa, in the company of the autistic and rejected Tiff, must solve the mystery of a man who just won't let his business go.

Corpse Reviver is the first murder mystery involving the formidable and sometimes downright rude lady of leisure and her straight talking niece. Bonded by blood, and thrown together by fate, join this pair of thrill seekers as they realise that flirting with danger brings a price to pay.

Highlands and Islands Detective Thriller Series

https://grjordan.com/
product/waters-edge

Join stalwart DI Macleod and his burgeoning new DC McGrath as they look into the darker side of the stunningly scenic and wilder parts of the north of Scotland. From the Black Isle to Lewis, from Mull to Harris and across to the small Isles, the Uists and Barra, this mismatched pairing follow murders, thieves and vengeful victims in an effort to restore tranquillity to the remoter parts of the land.

Be part of this tale of a surprise partnership amidst the foulest deeds and darkest souls who stalk this peaceful and most beautiful of lands, and you'll never see the Highlands the same way again

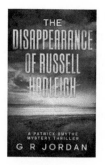

The Disappearance of Russell Hadleigh (Patrick Smythe Book 1)

https://grjordan.com/product/the-disappearance-of-russell-hadleigh

A retired judge fails to meet his golf partner. His wife calls for help while running a fantasy play ring. When Russians start co-opting into a fairly-traded clothing brand, can Paddy untangle the strands before the bodies start littering the golf course?

In his first full novel, Patrick Smythe, the single-armed former policeman, must infiltrate the golfing social scene to discover the fate of his client's husband. Assisted by a young starlet of the greens, Paddy tries to understand just who bears a grudge and who likes to play in the rough, culminating in a high stakes showdown where lives are hanging by the reaction of a moment. If you love pacey action, suspicious motives and devious characters, then Paddy Smythe operates amongst your kind of people.

Love is a matter of taste but money always demands more of its suitor.

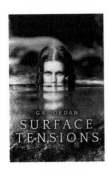

Surface Tensions (Island Adventures Book 1)
https://grjordan.com/product/surface-tensions
Mermaids sighted near a Scottish island. A town exploding in anger and distrust. And Donald's got to get the sexiest fish in town, back in the water.

"Surface Tensions" is the first story in a series of Island adventures from the pen of G R Jordan. If you love comic moments, cosy adventures and light fantasy action, then you'll love these tales with a twist. Get the book that amazon readers said, "perfectly captures life in the Scottish Hebrides" and that explores "human nature at its best and worst".

Something's stirring the water!

9 781914 073601